WIN HADLEY SPORT STORIES

WINNING PITCHER (*A baseball story*)

"KEEPER" PLAY (*A football story*)

OVERTIME UPSET (*A basketball story*)

SET POINT (*A tennis story*)

SLASHING BLADES (*A hockey story*)

DUEL ON THE CINDERS (*A track story*)

A Win Hadley Sport Story

SET POINT

BY MARK PORTER

SIMON AND SCHUSTER

New York, 1960

LIBRARY OF CONGRESS CATALOG CARD NUMBER:
60–8133
MANUFACTURED IN THE UNITED STATES OF AMERICA
BY H. WOLFF BOOK MFG. CO., INC., NEW YORK

CONTENTS

CHAPTER		PAGE
1	*To Play or Not to Play*	7
2	*Win's Decision*	15
3	*The "Old Man"*	23
4	*The First Lesson*	29
5	*The Storm on the Wyandot River*	37
6	*Dan Slade Loses His Boat*	51
7	*Good Advice from Ed Partridge*	58
8	*Matt's Humiliation*	67
9	*Win Faces an Expert*	75
10	*A Doubles Match*	85
11	*Another Doubles*	98
12	*An Interlude*	107
13	*Scoop's Pink Bomb*	113
14	*An Uneasy Victory*	120
15	*Dangerous Passengers*	132
16	*A Strange Trip*	151
17	*Captain Logan Takes Charge*	157
18	*A Trap Is Sprung*	171
19	*The Semi-Finals*	188
20	*The Finals*	210
21	*From Tennis to Croquet*	219

CHAPTER ONE

To Play or Not to Play

MATT HIT THE BALL HARD; it went fast into Win's backhand corner. Win stepped into it, hitting the ball crisply, the racket coming around level and flat. Matt started after the return, lunged, then tripped and fell. He rolled over, put his racket gently on the ground, crossed his arms over his chest and closed his eyes.

Win leaped the net and ran over to him.

"Hey," he said, "are you hurt?"

"Please," said Matt, "I just want to rest in peace."

"Are you hurt?"

"I'm too stupid to hurt," said Matt, and rolled over and got up. He stood there panting a little, his strong, stocky legs covered with clay from the court. He began to brush himself off. "Son," he said, "you're too good for me. I'm just a strong, dumb tackle. For this game you have to be fast."

Win grinned at him and brushed the dirt from Matt's back. He patted the strong shoulders. "You're right," he said; "at least about being dumb."

"You're too kind," said Matt. "Winner buys."

"Winner buys what?"

"One large, expensive milkshake, heavy on the ice cream."

"Since when?" asked Win.

"Since now," said Matt. "A new rule; I just made it up. Very good rule, don't you think?"

Win laughed. He felt good. It had been a fast workout and he could feel his timing was almost right. He was breathing easily and the clear spring air came cool into his lungs. "All right," he said, "but we'll have to split. I'm a little short this week. I lost a couple of million on the stock market."

"It's been a rough week," said Matt. "I know just how you feel. However, I accept."

They put on their sweaters, covered their rackets and went off down the street—Win, tall and wiry, with slim hips and good shoulders; Matt, much heavier but a little shorter, with a powerful man's body.

They headed for the Dixboro Malt Shop near the high school and, as usual, found a lot of their friends there. They sat down in a booth and ordered one milkshake and two glasses.

A slight, thin boy walked over to their booth and looked at them with bright, intelligent eyes made owlish by a pair of thick glasses. "Ah," he said, "the gladiators. An honor, I say, a veritable honor—an appearance in the midst of the peasants. I request an audience, no, I beg an audience."

"My gosh," said Matt, "what are you talking about?"

"Hi, Scoop," said Win, "sit down." He moved over to make room.

George ("Scoop") Slocum was a brilliant student. He was almost certain to be the valedictorian of the class and already his column on sports in the school paper was good enough so that the Crawford *Record* occasionally gave him an assignment.

"I love to talk to you, Scoop," said Matt, "even if I can't understand what you're saying."

"That's all right, lad," said Scoop. "I don't always understand myself."

"What a relief," said Matt. "That's what I thought."

They all grinned at one another.

"Now," said Scoop, "enough of this idle chitchat. This is official." He turned to Win. "Consider this an interview for the *Dixboro Diary*. I want your opinion on your chances of winning the State Juniors this year."

"Very small," said Win, "since I'm not even going to enter."

Scoop stared at Win. "You're joking!"

"No, he isn't," said Matt. "I've been arguing with him all day."

"Well, why not, for heaven's sakes," said Scoop. "You went to the quarter finals last year, and it took the guy who won it to put you out. Heck, he won't even be in it this year; he's too old."

"I know," said Win, "but I've got to work this summer."

"Work? You worked last year and still played."

"I know it," said Win, "but the foreman didn't like it much either. I almost got fired for taking the time off."

"Well, get another job," said Scoop. "This is serious. You know who'll win it if you don't enter, don't you?"

"A lot of people could win it," said Win. "Ralph Bates or Fred Atchison from Crawford, Willy Smith from Edgartown—a lot of them."

"Oh, come on," said Scoop, "you know who I mean. Dan Slade, that's who."

"Well," said Win, "I don't know why he shouldn't; he's a darn good player."

"He's not as good as you are," said Matt, "and you know it."

"You know it maybe," said Win. "He's very good—there's no question about that."

"He ought to be," muttered Matt; "he can play all the time with the pro at the country club."

Win turned toward his friend. "What's the difference? No matter how he does it, he does it, and he's good."

"Well," said Scoop, "we can't have this. I don't like it at all. Talk to him, Matt."

"The reason my face is this color," said Matt, "is because I've been talking myself blue. It's no use; he won't listen."

"I don't get it," said Scoop. "Don't you want to enter?"

"Of course I do." Win's face, thin and handsome, set in somber lines. "I want to very much."

"Well then?"

"I just think I ought to help out at home," said Win. "My brother is the only one that works and I think I ought to help, that's all."

"What does your mother think?" asked Scoop.

"I told her this morning," said Win, "and all she said was that I should do what I thought was right."

"Well," said Matt, and his voice was disgusted, "if you let Dan Slade win that tournament, I'm going to be sick."

"That's right," said Scoop. "I'll go even further. I'll go to Tibet and be a wise man sitting on top of a mountain thinking grim thoughts about my old friend, Win Hadley, who let the powers of darkness triumph because he wouldn't lift a hand—or a racket."

Win laughed out loud. "Dan Slade isn't exactly the powers of darkness. Anyhow he might beat me if I did enter."

"Never," said Matt. "Never in a million years."

"Hey, Matt," said Scoop, "how about getting your temptress sister after the lad? Maybe that would work."

Matt grinned. "We might try it. I'm sure Pat would be willing."

"Okay," said Win, a thin tide of red running into his face, "let's drop it, boys."

"Ah," said Scoop, "could it be our hero has a weakness? An Achilles' heel?"

"All right," said Win, "let's stick to the subject."

"All right," said Scoop, "let's. I think you're making a mistake. Not only because of Dan Slade, whom I personally consider a crumb, but because there is nothing wrong with winning a big tournament. You have a very good chance, and I think working this summer at a job where you can't get any time off is ridiculous. You can get another job; you don't have to work at the Slade sawmill."

"It's the best summer job in town," said Win. "Matt's working there too."

"That has nothing to do with it," said Matt.

"I'm no tennis player. Come fall, I'll take my strong back out on the football field and make like a hero again. But you're different, you're one of the best junior tennis players in the state, and I agree with Scoop that you're making a mistake."

"Maybe," said Win, "but that's the way it is."

"I'm disappointed in you," said Scoop, and pushed his heavy glasses back up his nose. "I was going to immortalize you in print. I refuse to write about Dan Slade."

"If you're going to be a good sports writer," said Win, "you have to, and you have to give credit where credit is due."

"I've heard of fair play," said Matt, "but this is ridiculous."

"You don't mean that," said Win; "I know you."

"All right," said Matt, "I admit it. But what Scoop says is right too. Leave Dan Slade out of it and I still think you ought to enter. A lot of people want you to."

"Listen," said Win, "I want to too, but I've made up my mind." He stood up and pushed past Scoop. "I've got to go; I'll see you guys later." He went out of the Malt Shop.

Matt and Scoop watched him go.

"I don't get it," said Scoop. "His family doesn't need the money so badly. It's not as if they were all that poor."

"I know," said Matt, "but you know Win. Since he doesn't have a father, he feels more responsible than the rest of us. He just feels he should help at home. It's the way he is."

"Well," said Scoop, and he sighed, "I guess we can't argue with that. But he would have won it for sure."

"Probably," said Matt; "but even if we don't like Dan, as Win said, he's a whiz at tennis."

Scoop looked at Matt for a moment. "Tell me something. What would you do in Win's place?"

Matt thought it over. "I don't know. Win's a little different, I guess. He's one of the best athletes they ever had at Dixboro, that's for sure, but he's not just a hunk of muscle. His trouble is he can think too." He smiled at Scoop. "Very dangerous combination, isn't it?"

"I couldn't say," said Scoop; "all I can do is think."

CHAPTER TWO

Win's Decision

On his way home, Win passed some younger boys that had been playing a loud, fierce game of baseball.

"Hey, Win," said one, a dirty little boy, hot and scuffed from his play, as he cocked his lightweight bat, "go ahead, throw one. I'll knock it out of the park!"

"I believe it," said Win, "you probably could." And he went on down the street, carrying his height and strength lightly and gracefully. The young boys trailed along with him, chattering, proud to be seen with him. They followed him all the way home, and as Win said goodbye to all of them, one at a time, their faces glowed.

Win walked into the living room and stopped in surprise. His brother, Walt, was sitting there talking to Tom Joyce, the head of the Physical

Education Department at Dixboro High School.

"There he is," said Walt, "our hero."

"Hello, Win," said Tom Joyce.

The coach was a well-built man, and his face was ruddy from the wind and the sun. He moved with the easy grace of a natural athlete and he gave an impression of physical competence, of strength. His extra weight was that of his years and not that of a fat man. His close-cropped, curly, gray-white hair was thick and his eyes were cool and gray.

Win's mother bustled in from the kitchen, wiping her hands on her apron. She stood on her toes and Win bent over and kissed her on the cheek. She was a plump woman with a quick smile. She looked at her young son. "All right," she said. "What is it?"

Win sniffed. "Beef, roast beef."

She threw up her hands. "What a nose," she said. "I don't think he ever misses." She stood back a little, studying Win. "I can't understand it, all he does is eat and he never seems to get fat." She sighed in mock dismay. "I wish I could say the same."

Win looked at her fondly. "You wouldn't look right skinny, Mom; I wouldn't recognize you if you lost weight."

"All right," she said, "for that you can have thirds. I know already you'll have seconds, so that doesn't count."

She turned to Tom Joyce. "I'm so glad you could come," she said, sitting down on the sofa with Walt. "There's no use beating around the bush. I believe in being direct." She sat back and looked at her older son.

"Yes," said Walt, "I guess you're right." He stood up and walked over to the fireplace and turned, his hands behind his back. "Win, we asked Tom to come over tonight for other reasons than a good dinner. We want to discuss the decision you've made. First let me say that Mother and I are proud of you. But we want you to know how we feel about it." He grinned at Win. "It may sound silly to say that it is your decision, with three formidable adults trying to change your mind; but it will be your decision finally. We asked Tom to come because he has some pretty good arguments too." He held up one finger. "First, we would like to make it clear that we want you to play in the State Junior Tournament. You might win it, but that's not even the point; we want you to have the chance. Second, it would be no financial hardship. Dad, before he died, made sure we would be taken care of, and, if I may say so, I'm doing very well in my job. So money is no great problem."

"But," said Win, "I'm sixteen now and I can earn my own money."

"Of course you can," said Walt, "and we have

another job for you where you can do both. We're not suggesting you don't work if you feel you have to."

"Another job?" Win stared at him. "What job?"

"Tom can tell you about that," said Walt. "He arranged it."

Tom Joyce stood up. "Before I tell you about that," he said, "I have something else to say." He looked at Win and his steady gray eyes never left Win's face.

"It's a funny thing about athletes," he said. "In a way they're a special breed of cat. People look up to them. We saw you come home surrounded by young lads who were proud just to be seen with you. Of course there is no reason that an athlete, just because of some accident of eye or muscle, should be a better person than somebody else— and often he isn't. But for some reason or other an athlete has some responsibilities to the people who watch him and look up to him. He is in the public eye; he becomes a bigger person than maybe he really is. Some of them are big enough for the job —and you are one of those, Win. We think you can enter this tournament and win—but even that is not the point. I think that being a good clean competitor is more important than the game itself, and when there is somebody who realizes that, the way you do, it would be a shame if he didn't compete." He smiled at Win suddenly. "I think you are embarrassed at all these compliments. But they're true nonetheless. You may feel that hitting a little white tennis ball is not too important, and in a way you are right. There are more important things in this life than sports." He paused for a moment. "If what you feel is lacking is responsibility," he went on, "you can find it in your athletics and in this tournament. Because you will have responsibility all right. To yourself, to your mother and brother, to me, and to the people who are watching you." He sat down again. "That's about it. I believe it's one of the longest speeches I've ever made."

Mrs. Hadley looked at her son with gentle eyes. "I think they've said everything. All I can add is that I think you should enter the tournament, and I am sure that your father would have wanted the same thing."

Win looked at the three adults in front of him. "It's not that I didn't want to play. I just wanted to do the right thing."

"Fine," said his mother, "and I'm sure you will."

"By the way," said Tom, "the job you'll have is pretty hard work, so don't think it'll be easy."

"What is it?" asked Win.

"You have to keep the public tennis courts in shape," said Tom, "and there are fifteen of them. They need work all the time."

"You mean for Ed Partridge?" asked Win, startled.

"That's right," said Mr. Joyce. "It's not the

Country Club but Ed keeps them in top shape, so if it's work you want you'll get it. You can start right after final exams."

"Hey!" Win was getting excited. "That's a *great* job! I've always wanted to work there. Maybe Mr. Partridge will help me with my game too."

"You'd better call him Ed," said Tom, and he smiled. "I don't think he would know who Mr. Partridge is."

"Golly!" Win began to pace the room. "This is great!"

"Don't get too excited," said Tom. "It's a lot of work and you won't get rich; but at least you can play in all the tournaments before the State Tournament."

"Work!" said Win. "That's not work. I'll be out there every day and I can play after I fix the courts."

"That's the plan," said Walt and looked with pleasure at his younger brother.

"Golly, Coach," said Win, "I don't know how to thank you."

"Don't bother," said Tom, his gray eyes sparkling. "I wouldn't have done it unless I wanted to. Besides, you can thank me by winning the tournament."

"Oh," said Win, sobered a little, "that won't be easy."

"Of course not," said Tom. "Who said it would be?"

"All right," said Mrs. Hadley, "let's eat. So much talk has made me weak."

Tom laughed. "I could have just finished a ten-course meal and I could still eat your food," he said.

Mrs. Hadley blushed with pleasure.

"I have to call Matt," said Win; "I'll be back in a minute." And he rushed into the hall where the telephone was.

"Hey, Matt," he said, when he heard his friend's voice, "hey, I'm going to enter the State Juniors!"

"What? Are you kidding?"

"Heck, no," said Win, and he told Matt all about it.

"Boy oh boy!" said Matt. "That Tom Joyce is a great guy!"

"And how," said Win. "Now I've just got to win."

"Quit worrying," said Matt; "you'll win."

"Maybe not," said Win, "but it won't be because I didn't try."

"Well, I don't mind if you lose the tournament as long as you can beat Slade before you lose."

"I said I'd try," said Win, "and that goes for Dan Slade, too."

"Beat him just because he's a crumb," said Matt.

Win laughed. "That's no reason. Shame on you, Matt."

"That's twice you've bawled me out today," said Matt, "and for the same reason."

"Oh, sorry," said Win. "But he's not really a crumb, he's just different, that's all."

"Well if he is, I'm glad," said Matt, "because I like being different from that guy."

"Just remember," said Win, "there are a lot of other players in that tournament besides Dan, and some of them are very good."

"Nuts," said Matt, and he chuckled. "If you can beat me, you can beat them."

"Okay, Bill Tilden," said Win, "if they're all as easy as you, it should be a breeze."

"Ho, ho," said Matt. "Wait 'til tomorrow, I'll run you to death."

"Okay," said Win; "your turn to buy new balls." And he hung up before his friend could answer.

CHAPTER THREE

The "Old Man"

SCHOOL WAS OVER, exams were finished, and, although Win felt he could have done better in Latin, he was, on the whole, satisfied with his grades.

As he walked the half mile to the public courts to start his new job, the warm thread of a summer breeze was in the air. It was a beautiful Monday morning and there was still a slight ground fog which the sun's rays crossed and silvered and caused to gleam. The streets were already shaded with late spring foliage and the white houses reflected the bright, slanting, early morning sun.

When he got to the Dixboro public courts, Ed Partridge greeted him shortly and put him right to work, rolling and lining the clay courts.

Ed Partridge was a man in his fifties whose one love was tennis. He was an old tournament player, he had won several state tournaments in his day, and now he worked for the town of Dixboro where his big responsibility was the care of the tennis courts. He was proud of them and he kept them in beautiful condition. He seemed unfriendly until you knew him. He didn't waste his words, he talked roughly sometimes, but he certainly knew his tennis.

He put Win to work immediately and kept him at it until late afternoon. Tom Joyce had been right when he had said that it would be hard work. About four o'clock, Ed came out on the courts, which were smooth and hard from Win's labor. He carried Win's racket and his own.

"Okay, son," he said, "do you want to hit a few?"

"I sure would," said Win, and reached for his racket.

"Just a minute," said Ed. "I hear you're a tennis player."

"Well," said Win, "I can play, if that's what you mean."

"That's what I mean," said Ed. "I'll have to see it to believe it."

"Well, gee, Mr. Partridge," said Win, "you asked me."

"Who?"

"What?"

"The name is Ed," said Ed, "that's what they call me."

"Oh," said Win, "I'm sorry."

"Don't be sorry," said Ed, "just call me Ed."

"Okay, Ed."

"That's better." Ed's face lit up suddenly as he grinned like a young boy. "All right, we'll see what kind of a player you are. Tom Joyce says you're pretty good, but me, I have to see for myself."

Win was getting a little angry. "Well, give me my racket and we'll see."

"All right," said Ed and gave Win his racket. He smiled again and walked away onto the court.

Win stared after him, then went over to the other side. Who does he think he is? he thought. This old man, it'll be a shame to beat him.

They began to rally and kept at it for about half an hour. Win began to hit harder and harder, really leaning into the ball with his young strength, often hitting the ball down the line and out of Ed's reach. Finally, Ed came up to the net holding the balls.

"How about a set?" he asked.

"All right," said Win, "if you want."

"I want," said old Ed and walked back to the service line.

"Do you mind if I serve?" he said pleasantly. "After all I'm an old man."

"Sure," said Win, "go ahead; it doesn't make any difference."

"That's right," said Ed, "it doesn't make any difference."

But it did make a difference. From the very beginning, Win was in trouble, but it took him almost the whole set to realize what was wrong. It was quite different from when they were just rallying. Then Ed had hit the ball right to him, but now he was doing just the opposite. He ran Win from side to side and back and forth, and when Win rushed the net he passed him easily for a point. It became embarrassing, and Win got so mad he started to hit the ball with all his might. He made some great shots, but he made a lot more errors. In about twenty minutes it was all over and Ed, that old man, had won 6–2 and he wasn't even breathing hard.

They went over to a bench and sat down, and Win couldn't even look at Ed, he was so ashamed.

Ed was quiet for a minute, then he said, "Don't worry about it, son, you just have a lot to learn."

"I guess so," said Win, staring hard at the ground.

"Maybe I was too hard on you," said Ed, "but if it will make you feel any better, you're the best junior I've seen around here in a long while."

Win's head jerked up. "Are you kidding?" he said. "I didn't have a chance. And with an—" He stopped just in time.

"With an old man?" said Ed, and he chuckled.

"That's all right, son, I *am* an old man. Certainly where tennis is concerned I am. But I'm not a dumb old man, and if there is one thing I know it's tennis. And I tell you, Win, you can be a very fine tennis player. You can hit, you have the strokes, you're quick, you have the will to win—and that's about all there is to it."

"But I lost," said Win.

"That's right," said Ed, "you lost. You lost because you're young and eager and you don't play the percentages. Headwork! Putting the ball where the other guy isn't. Right now, at sixteen, you have a better serve and a better forehand than I have. By that I mean the power and stroke is better. But if you continue playing the way you do, I will always beat you—and so will any smart tennis player."

"What do you mean?" asked Win. "What did I do wrong?

"Good," said Ed, "that's the first good move. You asked what you did wrong and that means you are willing to learn. Well, you did a lot of things wrong. You serve too many doubles, you overhit the ball, you try for the big shot all the time. It's fun to do that, maybe, but it isn't winning tennis. Sure you made a lot of mistakes, but the kind that can be corrected. The one thing you do have, I could never teach you."

"What?" asked Win. "What is that?"

"The ability. The co-ordination, the natural ability for the game. I have taught a lot of good players and, believe me, they started with less than you. But—" and he held up his hand—"that's only the beginning. You have to listen and work hard, or a lot of tennis players with less ability will beat you. It happens all the time."

"I'll do anything you say," said Win.

"I hope you mean it," said Ed, "because this is about the last friendly talk we're going to have. By the end of the summer when the State Juniors start, you'll probably wish you had never come over here. I'm going to work you near to death, son, and I'm going to do it because I think you're worth it." He looked hard at Win. "Don't disappoint me; I've waited a long time for a kid like you."

"I won't," said Win, and he really meant it. He believed this gray-haired old professional.

"All right," said Ed, "let's go."

"Go?" Win blinked at him. "Go where?"

"Out on the court," said Ed. "Where else?"

CHAPTER FOUR

The First Lesson

So OUT THEY WENT and Ed had been telling the truth. He worked Win in the hot sun for another two hours, until Win's breath was a hard rasp in his throat. Once he stopped to ask for a break, and he saw old Ed standing on the other side of the net, breathing easily and watching him, and he turned away abruptly and went back to the service line.

"You're proud of that big serve!" shouted Ed. "Go ahead, hit it in twice; go ahead!" And Win tried, and it worked once in a while, but the second serve was usually out.

Ed beckoned to him and Win walked up to the net.

"All right," said Ed. "Do you know what percentages are?"

"Sure," said Win, gasping for breath.

"What?"

"Well, I guess it's the percentage of times you get the ball in."

"That's very good. Very, very good. What do you think your percentage on your serve is?"

"Bad," said Win, sounding angry.

Ed looked at him. "Don't get mad at me, kid," he said; "my serve always goes in."

Win took a deep breath. "Sorry. What should I do?"

Ed grinned briefly. "You've got to learn an American twist."

"A what?"

"An American twist for your second serve. What's the matter, aren't you patriotic?"

Win had to laugh, and then everything was much better. "Sure, I'm a real patriot. Let's learn the American twist."

Ed looked at him for a moment, and he didn't smile. "I think you'll do, Win," he said seriously. "I really think you'll do."

Win recognized the great compliment and he blushed with pleasure. He was learning that a compliment from Ed was very rare and not easily come by.

Ed showed him how to hit his serve with the American twist—with the racket cutting sharply across the ball, giving it a rapid spin and an erratic bounce. It wasn't easy. The racket was difficult to control and the first time Win tried it he hit the ball on the wood and knocked it clear over the fence.

But Ed kept him at it, and finally Win began to get some of them in the service court, and when he did they bounced high and at a sharp angle and Ed had trouble hitting the ball cleanly. But it was slow, hard work and Win missed a lot more than he got in.

"Keep at it," said Ed; "it's coming real well. Don't expect to get many in at first. It probably feels awkward now but it's something you have to learn."

It did feel awkward at first to Win. He was used to stepping into the ball and hitting as hard as he could. This was a different stroke entirely, but slowly the knack of it came to him although he still hit most of them out.

As he walked around the court retrieving the balls, he saw a big, shiny convertible pull into the parking lot next to the court. There were three people in the front seat and one of them was Dan Slade. They didn't get out; they just sat in the car and watched the two players on the court without saying anything. Win went back to the service line and began serving the balls in his old way, hard, as hard as he could. He hit about five of them and then Ed came up to the net and beckoned him over.

"What are you doing?" he asked.

"I just thought I'd practice some first serves for a while," said Win.

Ed studied him for a moment. "That's young Dan Slade in that car, isn't it?"

Win looked away from him. "Yes," he said.

"Are you serving for him or to learn something?" asked Ed.

"To learn something," said Win, but he knew very well what Ed meant.

"Win," said Ed, "I understand what you're doing, and now is as good a time as any to learn to forget the gallery. Serving with all your might may impress young Slade but it won't help you beat him. Go on back there and keep trying the twist." Ed spoke firmly, and when he finished he turned and walked away.

Win went back to the service line, turned, then threw up a ball. He was so tense now that he hit it on the wood and the ball flew wildly at an angle and hit high on the backstop.

There was a loud snicker from one of the boys in the car. Win's neck and face grew warm as a slow tide of red seeped into them. Doggedly, he hit another one. It was better, but it didn't come close to the service court. This time he heard some giggles. Angry, he smashed one without bothering with the twist. It went in and Ed didn't even try for it; he just stood there looking across the net at Win. Ed didn't say anything, but suddenly Win was a little ashamed of himself. Forget them, he said to himself; do what Ed tells you.

So he went back to hitting the twist serve, over and over again, and a slight smile appeared on Ed's face. Win hit a lot of them way out, and again the derisive snickers and giggles could be heard from the direction of the car. Win ignored them and kept practicing. Then, suddenly and clearly, he heard the hard voice of Dan Slade. "Be quiet!" he said to the other two in the car and it was clear that he was not joking. The noise stopped immediately and Win looked over at the car. The two other boys were sitting there looking somewhat uneasy, but Dan looked back calmly at Win. Win waved at him and Dan waved back.

Win went back to work but he was a little surprised. He had thought it was Dan laughing at him and he hadn't expected him to defend him like that.

Finally Ed called a halt. "You're getting it, I think," he said. "Just keep at it, you'll get it for sure." He smiled at Win "You seemed to learn something else too," he added. "I think you know what I mean."

"Yes," said Win, "those guys didn't really bother me."

"They didn't, huh?" said Ed.

Win had to laugh. "Well, maybe a little. At first."

"Tomorrow at eight," said Ed, and picked up the bag of balls and walked away.

Win covered his racket and put on his sweater. He went out the gate past the car.

"Hi, Dan," he said, ignoring the other two except for a slight nod.

"Hi, Win," said Dan. "You working here?"

"Yes," said Win, "on the courts for the summer."

"Going to enter the Junior?"

"Sure. Are you?"

"Of course. I ought to win it this year."

"You might," said Win; "it's possible."

"It sure is," said Dan, and started the car. "Working on an American twist, I see."

"That's right," said Win. "It's pretty tough."

"Not so tough," said Dan placidly. "I've got it down pretty well."

"Boy, I'll say," said one of the others. "You should have seen him up at the club. He was—"

"Shut up," said Dan.

The boy blinked. "Gee, Dan," he said, "I was just . . ."

"Just shut up," said Dan. "You heard me."

Win was embarrassed at the scene. He couldn't see why Dan was being so unfriendly to the boy who had complimented him.

"I hope you learn the twist," said Dan, "you're going to need it."

"That's what Ed said," said Win, "and I believe him."

"Old man Partridge?" said Dan. "I didn't think he knew enough to make a bright remark like that."

Win stared at Dan. "He knows more about tennis than anyone else around here."

Dan shrugged. "He's an old woman," he said; "he plays a sissy game."

"What do you mean?"

"That soft stuff," said Dan, "an old woman's game."

"Well, he could beat you right now," said Win; "that's for sure. No matter what kind of game he's got."

"Are you kidding? I could beat him left-handed."

"Well I *am* left-handed," said Win sharply, "and I couldn't beat him today."

"You mean you lost?" Dan laughed. "This tournament is going to be easier than I thought."

Win knew that Dan was just baiting him, but he didn't like what Dan was saying about Ed Partridge. "That's right, I lost," he said. "To a better man—and that's why I lost." He turned away. "So long," he said shortly.

As he walked down the street, the convertible went by him with a heavy *whoosh*. Win knew that Dan had to drive by his house but Dan didn't offer him a ride, and Win knew he wouldn't have accepted if he had.

He just didn't understand Dan Slade. He had made the two boys that were laughing shut up, yet later he had been downright unfriendly when Win had talked to him. Maybe it was having all that money, Win thought, and no real friends. Certainly the two with him were not treated like friends. It couldn't be just having more money than other people, that wouldn't make Dan Slade unpopular. Win thought the reason was probably Dan Slade's father, a big, talkative man, an ex-athlete, who wanted his boy to be the best at everything. And he was just about that too, Win admitted. He was an excellent athlete, and his grades were almost as good as Scoop Slocum's. Win shook his head slowly as he walked along. It seemed too bad. Dan had a lot of things in his favor, but he certainly went out of his way to irritate people. Maybe, because of his father, Dan tried too hard. No matter what the reason, Win thought it was a shame.

CHAPTER FIVE

The Storm on the
Wyandot River

WIN WORKED and played hard all week at the municipal courts. On Sunday, when all the courts were busy with the perspiring citizens of Dixboro, Win went for a sail in Scoop Slocum's twenty-one-foot sloop, the *Four Winds*. Matt Hughes and his sister, Pat, came along, and they took a picnic basket with them.

It was a blustery day, with a strong northwest wind pushing heavy feather clouds fast across the sky. Faintly, to windward, could be seen a long line of darker clouds, far to the north.

"Great day for sailing," said Scoop as they put their gear on board.

"Plenty of wind," said Matt. "I'm thankful I'm in the hands of a great sailor."

"Thank you," said Scoop, "you're absolutely right."

Matt was right. Scoop didn't bother much with
sports, but he was a first-class sailor and had often
taken his little boat well out into the Atlantic
which was where the Wyandot River emptied. He
loved his little white boat and kept it in fine condition. This was the first day it would be in the
water. Scoop had hauled it for the winter, but for
the last three weeks he had spent almost every day
at the boat yard, caulking, scraping and painting
the hull and tightening the standing rigging.

The sloop looked beautiful as it tugged rest-
lessly at its moorings, lying alongside the slip. Its
topsides gleamed with the new coat of white paint,
and the sails were already neatly furled.

Win was impressed, as always, by the knowledge
and efficiency of the sloop's skipper, Scoop.

Before they cast off, Scoop gave them a little
speech. It wasn't a bossy speech, but there was no
nonsense in his tone. He showed them all where
the life jackets were, and he assigned each one to
some specific task, and he ended by explaining
briefly what could happen if certain mistakes were
made. He smiled around at his makeshift crew
and then he started the little twelve-horse-power
auxiliary engine.

"Now hear this," he shouted, as if to a vast crew
on a big square-rigger. "Stand by to cast off!"

Matt and Win stood by the bow and stern lines
and Matt knuckled his forehead in the manner of

the old-time seaman. "Aye, aye, sir!" he shouted back. "Standing by, sir!"

They cast off and leaped aboard. Scoop steered the sloop skillfully away from the dock and they putted out of the little bay and into the broad Wyandot River. The wind had blown up a short chop on the water and Scoop ran a course that compensated for both the current and the wind. As they got out farther, the bow of the little sloop dug into the bigger waves, and spray flew over the boat, wetting the people on board. Fortunately the early summer day was warm and so was the water, so it was not too uncomfortable.

The wind was off their port quarter, and Scoop came into the wind temporarily while they ran up the mainsail and the jib. Then, with the boat leaning over on the port tack, they scudded downstream at a merry six or seven knots. Scoop shut off the auxiliary engine and it was suddenly very quiet, with only the chuckle of the water rushing past the hull and the strain and creak of the sails and rigging.

They headed for Bilk's Island about fifteen miles down the broad river. They arrived in about two and a half hours and anchored in the little cove, untied the dinghy and rowed to shore.

There Win built a driftwood fire and they had a picnic lunch served by Pat Hughes, who fussed over the boys as if she were a hostess at a dinner party. After the last frankfurter had been consumed and the last container of milk drained, they settled back comfortably against some logs and the talk turned to the State Junior Tournament.

"I'm glad you have a job that'll let you enter, Win," said Scoop, pushing his glasses back up his nose. "Now I can be your personal public relations man."

"You're very kind," said Win, "but remember there are others in that tournament."

"I suppose you mean Dan Slade," said Scoop. "Well you know how I feel about him."

"I've been meaning to talk about him," said Win thoughtfully. "You know, I think we're too hard on him. I don't think we give him much of a chance. I think he's just lonesome."

"Lonesome?" Matt snorted. "With that car? And all that money?"

"I think Win's right," said Pat, her pert face wrinkling a little in thought. "I know him a little, and I always find him very polite and very nice. The way you all talk he's some sort of monster."

Matt rolled over, shifting his position. "All right," he said, "seriously, I just don't like the guy, and I'm not even sure why. Of course he's not a monster, Pat, in fact he's good at a lot of things, I know that. But I still don't like him."

"Hear, hear," murmured Scoop. "My sentiments exactly."

"We might be a little jealous," said Win. "Who wouldn't like to have a car and good grades besides?"

"Jealous!" Matt laughed. "Of that creep?"

"Shame on you, Matt," said Pat. "I say we don't give him a chance to be friendly."

"All this psychology is too deep for you little children," said Scoop blandly. "If you want a first-rate professional diagnosis of Dan Slade's sad case, Dr. Scoop Slocum would be happy to oblige." He sat up and took off his glasses and held them in his hand, using them for emphasis, and scowling seriously and stroking an imaginary beard. "Yes, my children, primarily young Slade is suffering from a basic insecurity syndrome stemming from an Oedipal rivalry with the male sire." He put his glasses back on and leaned against his log.

"Wow!" Matt stared at him. "I don't know what it means but it certainly sounds very serious. Maybe we should operate."

"I don't know what it means either," said Win, "unless Scoop is saying that his father pushes him too hard."

Scoop turned his head and looked at Win. "Bravo!" he said. "Go to the head of the class, Win. That's exactly what I do mean."

"In other words," said Pat, "he tries too hard to succeed. And it shows, so you boys don't like him."

"Well, what the heck," said Matt. "Win tries to win too, and everybody likes him."

"Yes," said Scoop, "but what Dr. Hadley is saying is that there is a way to do it. After all, my young friends, remember—if someone wins, someone also loses. So you've got to learn how to win and also how to lose because you don't do either one all the time."

"Where did you learn all this?" asked Matt.

Scoop sighed in mock impatience. "Brilliance, my dear Hughes, sheer native brilliance." He sighed again. "Sometimes it's too much for me too, but I have to live with it."

They all laughed and Matt threw a tired piece of frankfurter bun at Scoop, hitting him on the cheek.

Scoop picked it up and frowned at it. "Genius," he said. "No one understands. I am being stoned for my genius."

"Okay," said Win, and stood up, "enough of this nonsense. I think we'd better start back or we won't make it before dark."

Scoop looked up at the sky.

"Oh, oh," he said, "I'm a failure. I didn't notice. Look." He pointed off to the north, and they all looked.

Several miles off, but moving noticeably, was the long line of dark clouds they had seen when they had started out that morning. They were much closer now and they were dark and angry looking.

"The wind's backed around a little too," said Scoop; "we'll be going right into it on the way back. We'd better go back under sail and power. At least with the tide coming in there won't be much current against us."

They put out the fire carefully, pouring on several buckets of water to be certain there were no sparks left, and cleaned up the area. They climbed carefully into the little dinghy and rowed back to the anchored sloop.

As the clouds moved toward them, the wind rose and the water got increasingly rough. They were beating back to windward, and under sail alone they would have made only about three or four knots, but with the auxiliary going they were making at least six.

The little sloop leaned hard over on the starboard tack. The short, choppy waves smacked into the bow and the air was full of flying spray and, at times, sheets of water.

Pat stayed below in the little cabin, out of the wet, but the others stayed on deck and trimmed the sails at Scoop's orders in an effort to get the most out of the strong wind. There was no danger, especially with Scoop at the helm, but it was certainly uncomfortable.

They were about two miles from the dock when Win suddenly spotted another sailboat on the same tack coming in at them from an angle. He pointed it out to Scoop who turned and studied it for a moment.

"He shouldn't be out in this weather," he said. "That's just a little centerboard boat, a Lightning Class, I think. He could capsize easily."

"Hey," said Matt, "what about us?"

"That's different," said Scoop. "This boat has a three-thousand-pound keel on it. It's like a cork with a nail—it will always right itself. But that little thing is just a hull, and the weather is much too heavy for it." He watched as the other boat came rapidly near. "Speak of the devil. It's Dan Slade. He'd better get back to shore before that line squall hits."

It was Dan Slade, alone in his long, slim little boat. He was hiking out—that is, keeping the boat balanced mainly with his own weight, and the boat was scudding along very fast.

"How about a race?" he shouted as soon as he got near enough.

"Go in, Dan," shouted Scoop. "The weather's getting worse. You'll capsize in that thing!"

"Not me!" hollered Dan. "Come on, let's go!"

"Nothing doing," said Scoop, and he leaned over and throttled down the engine and turned into the wind. The sloop lost way and slowed down to about two knots.

"What the heck," said Matt, "let's race him."

"We can't do that," said Scoop. "He can go

faster with that hull than we can, but anyhow it's too dangerous for him."

"What are we slowing down for?" asked Win.

"We can't leave him out here alone," said Scoop. "If he goes over in this water, he may stay there. There's no one else around."

Win looked around him. The black clouds were almost overhead and the wind had come up until it was whistling through the standing rigging. The water was choppy, with odd currents and whirlpools moving without pattern and sometimes against the current. Its color was dark and mean and gray. They were far from shore and Win could see the danger for somebody in the water trying to hold onto a capsized boat.

He waved at Dan. "Go on in!" he shouted.

"Chicken!" Dan's voice trailed away as he passed their bow and came about on the port tack and started back.

"He's nuts," said Scoop, "but he sure can handle that boat."

"He's all right, then," said Matt.

"No, he's not," said Scoop. "I don't know what he's trying to prove out here. He could drown and I'm not kidding."

"Well, what'll we do?" asked Win.

"We'll just have to keep him as near as possible," said Scoop, "at least until he gets in."

"What if he doesn't go in?" said Matt.

"Then we don't go in," said Scoop. "I'm telling you he's a fool but he'll be a drowned fool if he keeps this up." He revved up the auxiliary and took off after Dan.

The little boat was going just off the wind and it was going several knots faster than the sloop, its light hull sliding over the waves instead of through them as Scoop's deeper draft keel boat did. Dan got farther and farther away but at least he was going shoreward. They followed him for over a mile.

"Oh, oh!" said Scoop suddenly.

They all looked—and the sail of the other boat had disappeared.

"He's gone over," said Scoop. "Put on your life jackets, and get a life ring ready on a line." He opened the motor full and as the sloop responded he said, "Get the sails down and stop them, this squall is due any second."

Matt and Win, working together, brought down the big main and jib, and as they were tying them down, the squall hit and hit hard.

The wind velocity almost doubled and a heavy cold rain dropped suddenly in driving sheets straight into their faces. The sky darkened, the light fading suddenly, and the visibility became so poor they could scarcely see the shore.

"Keep your eyes peeled," said Scoop, raising his voice over the noise of the wind and rain; "he won't be easy to see and we don't want to miss him. Watch out for the white sail lying on the water."

It was Matt who saw him first. "There he is!" he shouted, pointing.

Lying almost dead ahead in the water was the capsized boat, with Dan Slade's head a black dot near the hull. He was holding on and waving at them. That it was difficult to hold on was evident. The hull was constantly caught in the currents and eddies, sometimes spinning around in circles for several moments.

Scoop brought the sloop into the wind, skillfully maneuvering to within two or three feet of Dan.

"Throw him the life ring!" he shouted, and Win tossed it into the water right next to Dan.

"No," shouted Dan. "Throw me a line, so we can tow my boat in!"

"We can't!" shouted Scoop. "It'll be too much of a drag; we won't make any speed!"

Dan picked up the life ring and cast it aside. "Then don't bother! I'll bring it in myself!"

"Can he do it?" asked Win.

"Of course not, the idiot," said Scoop. "He's tired right now just from holding on. Look at him bounce."

Not only Dan but the sloop, stopped in the water, was bouncing all over the place. The motion was fierce, and the boys on the sloop had to hold on all the time to keep from being pitched over the side and into the water with Dan.

"Come on, Dan!"

He ignored them. He was trying with no success to right his capsized boat by pulling with all his strength and weight on the gunwale, but it was impossible. It would have been hard enough on a calm day; in this weather there was no hope.

"What'll we do?" asked Win. "He won't listen."

"I don't know," said Scoop. "We can wait until the squall passes, but from the looks of it, it's going to be some time before it does."

"All right," said Win, "throw him a line for his boat."

"We can't tow that thing," said Scoop. "With that wet sail in the water it's like being tied to a dock."

"I know," said Win, "but if that's the only way to get him on board we'll have to do it." He turned back to Dan.

"Okay, Dan! Here's a line for a tow rope!" Win threw a coiled line out to Dan, who grabbed it and tied it onto the mainsheet traveler. Then he grabbed the life ring which had luckily floated near, and Win and Matt hauled him aboard. He flopped over the gunwale and lay on the deck, streaming water and exhausted.

"You all right?" asked Win.

"Sure," said Dan, gasping for breath, "of course."

"Of course," said Matt, but fell silent when Win glanced at him.

"Now what?" asked Scoop. "Do we sit out here? We can't tow it."

Dan sat up. "What do you mean you can't tow it? You've got an auxiliary, haven't you?"

"Look," said Scoop, "this is my boat and I know what it will do and what it won't. It wouldn't tow that tub of yours twenty yards in an hour—not in this weather and with your sail lying there in the water. It would be hard to steer too."

"Don't be dumb," said Dan. "We can't just sit here."

"Why can't we?" asked Matt. "Until the storm blows over. Then we can do something."

"He's right," said Scoop, "about not sitting here, I mean. We're drifting, and if we drift far enough we'll go on the rocks near that spit." He pointed. "And if that happens, brothers, it's good-bye boat."

"Well, keep the auxiliary going," said Dan, "and maybe we can hold our own."

"That's about it, I guess," said Scoop, and then he frowned. "I hope that line doesn't break."

They all looked at the line securing Dan's boat. As the boats bounced up and down, and pitched and rolled, the tension on the line was enormous.

"I'll put some chafing gear on this end so it won't wear through on the gunwale," said Scoop, "but there's nothing I can do about the other end."

Dan staggered to his feet. "I'll go over the side and check it," he said.

"Oh, no, you won't," said Win. "You're so tired now you can hardly move."

"Whose boat is it?" snapped Dan.

"I don't care whose it is," said Win. "You're not going back in that water."

"Says who?"

"Says me," said Win. "And if I have to beat you up to keep you from being stupid, I don't mind at all."

"There it goes!" shouted Scoop and everyone on board staggered and held on as the sloop suddenly leaped forward in the water. The line had parted at Dan's boat's end, and the little boat was floating free and drifting rapidly downstream toward the rocks jutting out from the spit of land where the river curved.

"My boat!" cried Dan. And before anyone could stop him, he leaped over the side and into the churning gray water.

CHAPTER SIX

Dan Slade Loses His Boat

WIN RUSHED TO THE GUNWALE and stood there indecisively for a moment. Dan was going downstream rapidly, and the sloop, freed of its tow, was going the other way.

"Wait!" snapped Scoop. "Wait'll I come around."

He threw the helm hard over and the little sloop came about and started downstream after Dan. They reached him in a few moments.

He raised his face to them and it was stamped with strain and effort. He was having a hard time of it and he would never reach his boat; it was going as fast as he was.

"If you're going after him," said Scoop in a calm voice, "tie a line on yourself first." He could tell by looking at Win what he was going to do.

It was apparent to all of them that Dan was too tired to keep afloat much longer.

Matt quickly tied a line around Win's waist, and over the side went Win, into the nasty dark water.

Scoop had kept his boat a few feet from Dan, maneuvering carefully so there was no danger from the boat's propeller either to the swimmers or to the line tied to Win.

"Come on!" gasped Win when he reached Dan. "Grab hold of the line!"

Dan was swimming weakly but he answered, "No, I'm going after my boat!"

"Quit wasting time!" said Win angrily. "Grab hold!"

"Nuts!" said Dan and tried to swim away.

"Okay," said Win grimly, "you asked for it!"

He swam up to Dan who, by now, was too weak to make much of a struggle, and put a strong arm around his neck from the rear. Dan thrashed feebly for a moment, then relaxed, and Win knew he was making it as easy as possible for him.

"Haul away!" shouted Win, and Matt began to pull them in.

It was hard work. The swirling water sucked and pulled at their clothes, and the choppy waves broke over their heads, filling their mouths with acrid water. Scoop took the sloop downstream past the two in the water, so Matt at least was hauling them in with the current instead of against it. When they were alongside, Scoop cut the motor and let them drift while he rushed forward to help Matt pull Dan over the side. It was hard work, the sloop was bobbing and rolling; but finally Dan and Win were on the deck looking like two exhausted fish that had given up the struggle.

Scoop went back to the helm, revved up the auxiliary and got under way.

"Go after my boat!" gasped Dan, barely able to breathe.

"Holy cow," said Matt, "don't you ever quit?"

"You're letting my boat go on the rocks!"

"There's nothing we can do," said Scoop. "You know that, Dan. We've tried everything." He looked to windward. "This storm is getting worse instead of better. We'd better get in ourselves; it's no fun out here."

"Go after my boat!" insisted Dan. "I'll pay you for your trouble."

Win looked at him coldly. "Why don't you be quiet?" he said. "You got yourself into this and you've caused us a lot of trouble."

"Tough," said Dan, and got to his feet. He scanned the water aft. "It's gone," he said, "I can't see it. Thanks a lot for all your trouble. You have a little trouble; I lose a boat."

"All right," said Matt, and walked up to him,

holding onto the rigging to keep from falling. "All right, you've said enough, Slade. One more word will be too much."

Dan studied him for a moment, then set himself as well as he could against the violent motion of the boat. "Okay," he started to say, and Matt went after him, but Win stepped between them.

"Come on," he said, "quit acting like kids. We've had enough trouble for one day."

Just at this tense moment, the hatch of the cabin opened and Pat Hughes put her head out. "Aren't we in yet?" she asked innocently.

They all stared at her. They had forgotten all about her in the excitement of the last hour. She glanced at Dan, then did a double take. "Dan Slade," she exclaimed, "what on earth are you doing here?"

Scoop slowly began to laugh, then everybody on the boat joined in except Dan, who sat on top of the cabin looking at them sourly. Between fits of laughter, Win explained what had happened.

"Darn it," said Pat, "I fell asleep on one of the bunks. I always miss the excitement." Then, not knowing how Dan felt, she made the mistake of asking, "Where's Dan's boat now?"

"They let it go on the rocks," said Dan; "they wouldn't even try to get it."

"Oh, stop that," said Scoop. "You know enough about sailing to know we did everything we could."

"What's my father going to say?" said Dan suddenly, and for a moment he looked very worried.

Nobody said anything, but they felt a little embarrassed.

When Dan spoke again he was in control of himself.

"All right," he said, "the boat's lost; especially if it went on the rocks it'll be a wreck. Okay. That's that. But don't think I'll forget it either. I'll get my chance, you'll see." He looked at Win and Matt. "Just remember that. If I get a chance to show you smart guys something I'll do it, that's for sure."

Win shrugged. "I'm sorry you feel that way, Dan, there's no reason for it."

"You say," said Dan, "but I've told you, so don't be surprised at anything."

"I wouldn't ever be surprised at anything you did, Slade," said Matt.

"Matt, hush," said Pat.

"Hush, smush!" snapped Matt, and he was angry. "We pull the guy out of the river in the middle of a big storm, we try to save his boat and *he* gets mad. What is he—nuts or something?"

"Never mind, Matt," said Win, "we can't help how he feels." He turned to Dan. "If you're worried about your father, we'll be glad to tell him how it happened. It was just one of those things."

"No, thanks," said Dan. "Do you know what that boat costs?"

"Who cares?" said Matt, still angry. "What's that got to do with anything?"

"Plenty," said Dan.

"All right," shouted Scoop, "we're coming in! Stand by to dock!"

They slid into their slip and tied the boat up carefully with extra mooring ropes and spring lines, because of the storm. Dan Slade didn't bother to help but he waited until they were finished.

"Hadley," he said, "I'm sure to be seeing you in some of the tournaments this summer. I want to wish you luck."

"Why, thanks," said Win, surprised.

"Because you're going to need it. I'm going to beat you as badly as I can." He turned and walked away down the dock, leaving the group staring after him.

"Boy," said Matt, finally, "he sure is one goofy guy!"

Win looked after the retreating figure thoughtfully. "I know," he said after a moment, "but for some reason I feel sorry for the guy."

"Well," said Scoop, his voice harsh from yelling over the storm, "you may be sorry for him, but I don't think he's sorry for you one bit. And if he meant what he said, I'd be careful. He's big and he's mean, and you can't tell what a nut like that will do."

Win shook his head slowly. "No," he said, "I don't think he's mean. I don't think he's a nut either. What he meant was that he'd beat me on the court and he could do it too, if I'm not careful." He smiled at his friends. "So, I'll just be careful!"

CHAPTER SEVEN

Good Advice from Ed Partridge

WIN'S FIRST SERVE, a real sizzler, was out about two inches. He bounced the second ball a couple of times, then threw it up and hit it, bringing the racket across the ball with a vicious slice. The ball went in a curve across the net, hit in the backhand corner and bounced like a rabbit, high and away.

Ed Partridge barely reached the serve and he couldn't hit it cleanly. The ball hit the wood of his racket and muffed into the net. He grinned at Win and came up to the net.

"That's the American twist all right," he said. "You've come a long way in a few weeks." He grinned at Win. "Your game and set, six–four. How do you feel now?"

Win smiled happily. "I feel good. That's the first time I ever beat you, Ed. You must have felt sorry for me."

Ed snorted. "Don't kid yourself, son. When I play it's to win. I lost because you got more points than I did. You're too good for me, Win, I'm not joking." He poked him with his racket. "But if I were your age, I wouldn't say that."

"Ed," said Win, "shall I enter the Dixboro Senior Tournament next week?"

"Of course," said Ed; "why shouldn't you? You might even go through a few rounds."

"You mean I might win it?" said Win jokingly.

"You might at that," said Ed; "sillier things have happened."

"Thanks," said Win, "thanks a lot."

"You're welcome," said Ed, and they both laughed.

"Who will win it?" asked Win as they went to the side of the court and sat down on a bench.

"Walter Williams," said Ed promptly. "No one around here can beat him."

"I've seen Mr. Williams play," said Win. "He sure is good."

"He's better than that," said Ed. "I saw him play in the Nationals at Forest Hills over twenty years ago, and he went all the way to the quarter finals and it took the winner to put him out."

"Golly," said Win, "I didn't know that."

"Sure," said Ed. "He wasn't a great player, but he was awfully close to it."

"Gee," said Win, "what if I draw him? It'll be awful!"

"Not really," said Ed. "It might be a good thing if you did. It won't hurt you to play against a first-rate player, a smart player, and Walter is certainly both."

"I wouldn't have a chance."

"Oh, he would probably beat you," said Ed, "but don't underrate yourself, Win. Remember Walter must be almost fifty years old now, and even though he's in good condition he just doesn't have your sixteen-year-old legs." Ed shook his head. "The legs always seem to go first. When you're your age it seems you can run forever, but Walter can just about make three fast sets and that's it. For the first set he's almost as good as he ever was, but then his legs start to go and he uses his head more, and that's where you could learn something from him. Somebody once said if you want to see a great match in any sport, watch a champion being beaten. That's really something. It took a lot for any champion to get to be one— besides his talent. It took drive and ambition and desire. And when he sees his crown slipping away, the fight he'll put up to keep it is really worth seeing. Walter is just the local champion, but he likes it and it'll take some doing to get him out of there for a few years at least."

"Well, it won't be me," said Win; "I've seen him play."

"It won't be you this year, but it could easily be you not too long from now."

"Wouldn't that be great!" said Win, then sobered. "But I think I'd hate to be the one to beat Mr. Williams if the time ever comes."

"Now that's ridiculous," said Ed, and he was very serious. "All champions have to step down sooner or later. That's the one certain thing about being one. And if you draw Walter Williams and don't try your darnedest he won't have the least respect for you. Especially if you had a chance to beat him. But don't worry, son; you aren't going to beat Walter this year unless he breaks a leg." Ed studied Win for a moment, a glint of amusement in his eyes. "I hear Dan Slade is entered too."

"Oh," said Win, trying to be noncommittal, "is that right?"

"That's right," said Ed. "Maybe you'll draw him. He's a very good junior player."

"I know," said Win.

"Do you think you could beat him?" asked Ed blandly.

Win turned and looked directly at Ed. "Yes, I think I could."

Ed laughed out loud and slapped Win on the knee. "I think you could too, son, if you paid attention to your knitting out there."

"Don't worry, I would."

"Well, Win, you're coming along pretty well so far. You still have some rough spots, but you're playing much better, much smarter tennis. You're using your head as often as your muscles and that's good tennis or good anything for that matter."

"Who do you think I'll draw?" asked Win. "With everybody eligible in town there are plenty of guys that could beat me."

"Some," said Ed, "but not plenty." He paused. "I don't know who you'll draw, but I'm on the committee and we're drawing tonight and making up the list of seeded players. I'll call you tonight and let you know. I see your friend Matt is entered too."

Win grinned. "Yeah, the old chowderhead. He might win a few himself. He never quits trying, that boy."

"That's one of the reasons he's a good athlete," said Ed. He stood up and put on his old sweater. "I've got to go, I'll call you tonight."

"Good night," said Win, "and thanks a lot, Ed."

"A pleasure, son," said Ed. "Try to remember some of the things I taught you when you get in that Seniors."

"I will," promised Win; "I don't see how I could forget."

"You'd be surprised," said Ed, "but let's hope not."

That night after dinner, Walt and Matt were playing Pat and Win a fierce, loud game of croquet when Mrs. Hadley called Win to the telephone.

"Hello?"

"Win? This is Ed Partridge. Are you sitting down?"

"Sitting down? No, why?"

"Maybe you'd better. I have the results of the draw."

"Oh-oh," said Win, "what happened?"

"First, Walter Williams, even though he's seeded number one, has to play a first-round match because of the unevenness of the number of entrants and because of the way the draw came out. Okay, that's not unusual, but guess who his opponent is?"

"Oh, no," said Win.

"Yes."

"Me?"

"You."

"Ouch."

"I agree. But remember what I told you. You can learn a lot playing against Walter. But that isn't all."

"Good gosh, it's enough, isn't it?"

"Well, we'll see, son. Your friend Matt Hughes." Ed paused.

"Yes, what about him?"

"And your other dear friend, Dan Slade?"

"Oh, not that!"

"Exactly that."

"Holy cow!" exploded Win. "It couldn't be a worse draw if it had been planned."

"Worse for whom?"

"For us, of course."

"How about the others? Remember, Win, this is competition. Draw or no draw you would have had to play one of the good ones sooner or later. It just happens to be sooner."

"Boy, first round," said Win. "How soon can you get?"

Ed laughed. "Well, I just wanted you to know the good news."

"Thanks a lot, Ed," said Win. "That was sure great news all right!"

Ed laughed again. "You're taking it very well, son. I congratulate you. Don't forget you're playing doubles with Matt. That's important too." He said goodbye and hung up.

Win walked slowly back out to the croquet court where they were waiting for him. He picked up his mallet and walked up to his ball and pretended to study the tactical situation. As he was judging the angles of a tough wicket shot, he said casually to Matt who was standing nearby watching him, "Oh, by the way, Matt, that was Ed on the phone. You play Dan Slade in the first round Monday." He bent over to pull an imaginary twig from the path of his croquet ball.

"What?" shouted Matt. "What did you say?"

"A tough shot," murmured Win, getting down on his knees and sighting over the top of his ball.

"Stop that nonsense!" shouted Matt. "Did I hear you say I had to play Dan Slade in the first round?"

"What?" Win looked up and blinked. "What? Oh. Yes, my poor lad, that's what I did say."

"Wheeeew!" Matt sat down hard on the grass. "What a break! And I do mean for Dan Slade."

"Maybe you can beat him," said his sister.

"Not me," said Matt. "I don't like him, but at that game I can't beat him either."

"Who'd you draw, Win?" asked Walt.

"Walter Williams," said Win.

"Oh, oh," said his brother, "that'll be rough."

"It sure will be," said Win.

"Holy cow," said Matt, "we sure drew some beauts!"

"Well, good luck, Matt, old bean," said Win, "because you are going to need all you can get. Now me, I don't need any luck; all I need is about three more rackets. We're in the doubles too, don't forget."

"You might say that so far this summer our tennis career is not likely to be a smashing success," said Matt glumly. "Why couldn't we draw a couple of pushovers so we could get through a couple of rounds, anyhow?"

"What the heck," said Win. "Ed said we'd have to run up against the good ones sooner or later, but this time it's sooner."

"He's right," said Walt. "There's no meaning in beating somebody that's easy."

"The way Win and I are beating you two right now?" asked Pat too sweetly.

"Are you kidding?" said Matt, getting to his feet. "If the left-handed marvel would honor us with making his shot and missing it so we can get on with it? The winning, I mean."

"A pleasure," said Win, and bent over and stroked his ball cleanly through the wicket from a difficult angle.

Matt hit his forehead with the palm of his hand. "Wow," he said, "you'd better save that kind of luck for Monday afternoon, son, and while you're at it, spread a little of it on me!"

CHAPTER EIGHT

Matt's Humiliation

THE DIXBORO SENIOR TOURNAMENT was held at the country club courts. It was a beautiful setting, overlooking the broad Wyandot River, and surrounded by the carefully tended rolling green grass of the golf course. The courts were at one side of the clubhouse, and the center court was in full view of the members of the club and their guests from the second-floor terrace. There were several rows of bleachers set up especially for the tournament, near the center court, and although it was the first day of the tournament there were a good many young high school and college students sitting and watching the action.

Win was scheduled to play at five-thirty, the last match of the day, because Walter Williams, a lawyer by profession, was unable to play any earlier on a weekday.

Win arrived at three, however, because Matt

Hughes and Dan Slade were scheduled then and he wanted to see the match, and if possible, be of some help to his friend. When Win got there, Matt was on a side court rallying with an older boy, a sophomore in college. They rallied for several more minutes, then Matt came over to where Win was standing.

"Come to see the lamb led to the slaughter?" he asked.

"Oh, come on," said Win, "it's not that bad."

"It's worse," said Matt mournfully. "I'm not in Dan's class. He'll murder me."

"Well, give it a try," said Win.

Matt looked at him. "Just a minute, son," he said. "I said Dan was too good for me; I didn't say anything about not trying. The words aren't in this boy's vocabulary."

Win clapped him on the back. "That's my boy. Now you sound like the old Matt."

"I may lose," said Matt, and then laughed. "I *will* lose, no doubt, but before I do the fur will fly. Danny boy will know he's been in a match."

"Give it all you've got," said Win. "We'll all be rooting for you."

Matt gave him a snappy salute. "Yes, sir," he said, "we shall attack!"

"Carry on," said Win, and together they walked over to the big board where all the pairings were listed. Win looked at his bracket.

"You know," he said, finally, "I don't like to brag, but if Walter Williams weren't in my bracket, I might go all the way to the semis. After him there aren't too many tough players for several rounds."

"But he *is* in your bracket, and Dan Slade is in mine so—goodbye boys," said Matt.

"Yeah, I guess we can't get around that," said Win. He held out his hand. "Good luck, Matt."

Matt shook his hand. "Thanks." He walked off to the center court.

Win went over to the bleachers and sat down with Tom Joyce and Pat Hughes.

"What do you think, Win?" asked Tom, nodding out to the court.

Win shook his head. "No," he said. "I'd like to say he had a chance, but Dan's just too good for him. He'll have to work though, Matt won't make it easy for him."

"Oh dear," said Pat, "with all his friends watching, I hope it isn't too bad."

"Oh, it won't be that bad," said Win, but inwardly he added, " I hope."

Win watched Dan Slade as he and Matt warmed up before starting the match. He had to admit Dan looked impressive.

He hit the ball with beautiful strokes, crisply and with plenty of strength. He hit a few practice overhead smashes and his stroke was big and well-timed and the ball boomed off his racket. Please, said Win to himself, don't let it be too bad.

The match started and it wasn't bad—it was awful.

From the beginning, Dan Slade seemed to play as if the match had been scheduled for the sole purpose of making Matt Hughes an object of ridicule.

All Matt had in his favor was his great spirit, and Dan used this as a weapon. Time and time again he hit a high soft lob over Matt's head, and then, after Matt had dashed way back after it, he would drop a little tantalizing shot just over the net, and Matt, being the way he was, would make a great effort to get back up to get it.

By the end of the first set, which ended six–love in favor of Dan Slade, Matt was tired out, and his white tennis clothes were covered with light brown clay, the result of several hard spills in desperate efforts to get a ball just out of his reach. As they changed courts, Win turned to Tom Joyce.

"He doesn't have to do that," he said angrily. "Why's he making Matt look like a clown?"

Tom shrugged and looked thoughtfully out onto the court at Dan, standing there breathing easily, his shorts and shirt still clean and fresh. "I don't know, Win," he said finally. "It seems he has something against Matt. What is it? Do you know?"

"If anything, he should be grateful to Matt," said Win, and told Tom about the incident of Dan's lost sailboat. "That's the only thing I can think of. What's wrong with Dan—acting like this?"

"I don't know, Win," said Tom, his voice troubled. "It doesn't make much sense."

The second set started and for the first three or four games it was much like the first set. Matt ran all over the court trying for Dan's clever, subtle shots, and several times he fell hard again. He didn't say anything, he didn't even look at Dan, he just kept trying as hard as he could.

The people on the side lines were silent, watching the unequal struggle, puzzled at something they didn't quite understand. They knew something odd was going on, but what it was they weren't quite sure.

Then, for no reason, Dan lost his touch. Balls that had previously gone in were now dropping just outside the lines.

Slowly Matt began to get back into the set. He got back the hard way, the only way he knew, running hard and trying for every ball.

This was something the watchers could understand and they began to urge Matt on, clapping warmly when he made a point. Win and Pat were cheering openly as Matt finally squared the set at five–all. And in another desperate series of efforts he won the second set at seven–five, and the match was even.

"How about that?" said Win excitedly to Tom.

"He earned it," said Tom. "Dan's started to miss, not by much, but it makes all the difference."

"Do you think he'll win now?" asked Pat, her hands clasped tight together in her tenseness.

"I don't know," said Win, "Matt's pretty bushed."

Matt was certainly showing the effects of having used up so much energy. He stood at the service line, his chest heaving as he gulped much-needed air.

Scoop Slocum came rushing up to where Win was sitting. "What a write-up I'll give this," he said excitedly, "especially if Matt wins."

But during the first game of the third and final set, it was immediately apparent that Dan had regained the fine touch with which he had started the match. His shots were all going in now and Matt was too tired to get most of them back.

Matt's friends sat in silence, watching, getting gloomier by the moment.

On set and match point a curious thing happened. Dan dropped a soft little shot just over the net and Matt, who was back on the baseline, came tearing up and dived for it. The ball came off his racket and went straight down the alley line.

"Out!" called the umpire. "Game set and match to Mr. Slade, six–love, five–seven, six–love."

The crowd applauded politely, then fell quiet as Dan Slade walked up to the umpire's chair, waving a ball at him.

"It was in," he said clearly, and held up the ball. "Here's the chalk mark."

The umpire nodded and they went back to play the point over. Dan served a blistering service ace and this time it was really over. The two players came to the net and shook hands briefly.

Win turned to Tom Joyce.

"Now how can you figure that guy out? He does all he can to make Matt look bad, then on match point he reverses the umpire's call in Matt's favor. I don't get it."

"Well," said Tom, "Dan might not be the nicest boy in school, but no one has ever accused him of cheating, or of trying to get something for nothing. And there's much to be said for a boy that acts that way."

Matt came over to them then, and he was tired and dejected.

"I said lamb to the slaughter, and that's just what it was," he said dispiritedly.

"Nonsense," said Tom, "he's a better player, you know that. You took a set from him and you deserved it. You played as hard as you could and I for one would like to congratulate you." He held out his hand and Matt took it.

He grinned. "I guess you're right, Coach," he said, "I didn't really expect that much."

"I hope I do as well as you did," said Win. "I have to play in about fifteen minutes."

"Well I'll watch," said Matt, "if you'll get me a couch to lie on. I'm bushed."

"Gee," said Scoop, "and I was going to write up a great story on the new Bill Tilden, Matt Hughes."

They all laughed, and then from the officials' table near the center court, Win saw Ed Partridge waving at him.

"I'd better go, I'll see you later." He went over to the officials' table.

"We just got a telephone call," said Ed, and he was watching Win closely. "It was Walter Williams, and he can't get here until six-thirty. You're scheduled at five-thirty, and the committee allows a player to be fifteen minutes late. After that he forfeits the match. Unless the opponent is willing to wait or play it another time." He looked at Win. "What'll it be, son?"

Win hesitated just a moment. He knew that if he got by Walter Williams he might very well go far in this tournament.

"I'll wait," he said. "I don't want to win by forfeit. If I win I want to beat him on the court."

Ed studied him for several moments. "That's what I thought you'd say. Okay, it'll be at six-thirty then."

CHAPTER NINE

Win Faces an Expert

THE TALL, slim man walked out onto the court and up to the umpire's chair. "Mr. Hadley?" he said.

"Yes, sir," said Win.

The man held out his hand. "I'm Walter Williams. I want to thank you for waiting."

Win shook his hand. "It was a pleasure, Mr. Williams."

"I've seen you play for the high school," said the man, "football, basketball. You're quite an athlete, Mr. Hadley."

"Thank you, sir," said Win, feeling very pleased and a little confused at being addressed as Mr. Hadley.

The umpire leaned over from his tall chair. "Are you ready to warm up?"

"I am," said Mr. Williams and looked questioningly at Win. "I've held this lad up enough, I think."

"I'm ready," said Win, and they got some new balls and walked out onto the court.

As Win went back to the service line he saw Ed Partridge sitting in the bleachers with his friends and Tom Joyce. He waved his racket and Ed nodded.

From the moment they started to rally, Win could see he had never played anyone like Walter Williams. His shots had a negligent sort of power, and he always seemed to be in position for a shot. During the rally he only netted one ball and he hit directly to Win, never making him run more than one or two steps to reach the ball.

He did another thing that Win had never seen before. He hit the ball on the rise, before it reached the top of the bounce, and the result was a hard flat shot with almost no spin on it. It would hit the court and skid with a low bounce, instead of the nice high bounce, the result of a ball hit with a lot of English. It meant that Win had to get to the ball at least one step faster or it would skid past him.

Win was nervous, but not frightened. The nervousness helped him; it sharpened his reactions and he was hitting the ball well; his timing was good and the ball went sharply off the racket.

They warmed up for about ten minutes, then,

after they had practiced two rounds of service, the umpire leaned over and said, "Ready?"

"Ready," said Williams.

Win took a deep breath. "Ready."

They spun the rackets for service and Mr. Williams won the spin and chose to serve.

He went back to the service line, held up the balls and looked questioningly at Win.

Win nodded and Mr. Williams threw the ball up and hit it.

He hit it much harder than he had in practice, and the ball blurred into Win's backhand corner and past before he reacted. It was a clean ace; Win hadn't even touched it.

He went back to the other court, determined at least to hit the ball on the next service. He took an extra step into his backhand corner in order to get an extra jump on the ball.

The serve came, fast as before, but this time into the forehand court, and Win, who had leaned toward the backhand side trying to anticipate, was caught off balance. He retraced his direction as fast as he could, and hit a soft shot off the heel of the racket. Mr. Williams, coming swiftly to the net, reached up and almost casually hit a driving overhead far out of Win's reach.

Mr. Williams missed the first serve on the next point and his second was an American twist executed with such effectiveness that Win flubbed it off the wood of his racket and into the net. He had never seen a bounce so erratic. It hit and bounced high and at a tremendous angle away from him. He had been lucky even to get his racket on it.

The game point serve was another blistering ace, and as they changed courts, as they did on all odd-numbered games, Win could feel his face burning.

He got the balls and walked to the service line and served a hard driving ball. Mr. Williams didn't even swing, and it looked like an ace.

"Mr. Hadley," intoned the umpire impersonally, "you will please not serve until you have asked Mr. Williams if he is ready."

Win was embarrassed. He went to the net and said, "I'm awfully sorry, Mr. Williams."

Williams smiled. "That's all right, Mr. Hadley." He winked unexpectedly at Win. "Relax a little, Mr. Hadley," he said, "it may help."

Win stared at him and then went back to serve. He felt better immediately and he was very grateful to the friendly Mr. Williams.

He felt better and he played better too, but it was not enough with a player as good as Walter Williams. Win tried as hard as he could and it became a very good match to watch. There were still quite a few people who had stayed late to see Mr. Williams play, and they were also curious about Win who had a fine reputation as a junior player.

At one point, Win actually had a chance to take the first set.

He had fought his way to a four–all tie in games and it was his serve. He had been serving well, holding all his serves, but he was constantly in trouble struggling for the key points. The rest of his game was exceptionally good—he had made some stinging placements and several smashes, but on the important points Williams won more easily than he.

He went to deuce on his serve and as he prepared to serve again an idea occurred to him. Instead of serving his second serve with the American twist, he decided to serve it hard, like his first. He hoped it would catch Mr. Williams off balance. He missed his first serve and tried his plan.

Mr. Williams was caught off balance all right but Win's serve went out and he was down to game point on his serve. It was the extra point Mr. Williams needed and he took the game as Win, unsettled, double-faulted again. His opponent held his serve and that was the first set, six–four.

Win got ready for the second set feeling angry with himself. He had played very well, he knew it, as well as he had ever played—and he had lost the set anyhow. There had been only three or four key points in the set and he had lost all of them. Otherwise he felt they had played even. Win was convinced he could win in spite of the fine playing of his opponent. He decided to play for the big shots, the power shots, to change tactics, and if it worked, to sweep Mr. Williams through the set before he changed his own tactics. Win, still angry, was certain it would work. It sounded good to him, and the way he felt, he wanted to hit the hard ball, the big one. The other way hadn't worked.

He tried it from the beginning and it worked for about two games. He won the first two, the first one at love, and feeling strong and exultant, he kept it up in the third game. He lost that one, and he didn't win another game.

His hard drives started going out and it took him the whole set to figure out why. Then it came to him. Mr. Williams had changed his game too. He was giving Win returns that were low and soft with low bounces, and Win had to run hard for them and then was in the wrong position to really drive a low ball.

He realized the mistake he had made. It was the same mistake he had originally made against Ed Partridge many weeks before. Mr. Williams was simply outsmarting him, using his head and playing the percentages. Win had made some beautiful shots but Mr. Williams had made the points. The score was five–two before Win realized this.

He changed again in the last game, and played the game Ed had taught him. The game was a long one, going from deuce and ad again and again, but Win finally lost it. The set and match was over.

Win went to the net and shook Mr. Williams' hand.

"You play very well, Mr. Hadley," said Mr. Williams. "If you continue to improve, you will be very good indeed."

"Thank you," said Win. "I didn't give you much competition."

"Nonsense," said Mr. Williams. "The first set had me worried." He looked at Win for a moment. "What did you try there in the second set? You were doing better the other way, I think."

Win shook his head. "I should have known better," he said. "Ed Partridge told me not to play that way."

"Ed Partridge? If he's your coach you're very lucky. Ed knows what he's doing, there's no question about it."

They shook hands with the umpire and thanked him; then as they left the court, Ed Partridge came over. He shook hands with Mr. Williams. "Hello, Walter, I see you're still as good as ever."

Mr. Williams laughed. "Not quite," he said.

"You've got a fine young player here, Ed. Except for one lapse I can very easily recognize your fine hand."

"Yes," said Ed, looking at Win for the first time, "except for one lapse."

Win flushed. "I'm sorry, Ed; I thought it would work and by the time I knew it wouldn't, it was too late."

"You wouldn't have won anyhow," said Ed, unfeelingly, "but the first set was all right. We won't mention the second except to say that you figured out you were wrong all by yourself and went back to your real game. That's one good sign."

Mr. Williams clapped his arm around Ed's neck. "Don't be too hard on the lad, Ed, he's got real promise and you know it."

Ed grinned a little. "Of course I know it. I wouldn't be here if I didn't." He turned to Win. "I told you you'd learn something playing Walter. It's certainly no disgrace to lose to him."

"Of course not," said Win, "not in the least."

"Thank you," said Mr. Williams. "If I know you, Ed, the next thing this young man is going to sweat over is a better lob, and maybe more work on his volleying."

Ed laughed out loud. "I told you, Win. This man knows this game. That's next, all right . . . the lob and the volley."

"What's wrong with my lob and volley?" asked Win. "I use those shots."

"Not enough and not quite right," said Ed; "but we can all take things one at a time."

"Well, okay," said Win, "if you say so."

"Listen to Ed," said Mr. Williams; "you won't be sorry." He held out his hand to Win. "Thank you, young man, it's been a pleasure playing you. I'm sure it won't be a pleasure if I have to do it again."

Win grinned with pleasure. "Thank you, sir."

"Ed." Mr. Williams shook hands with Ed.

"Thanks for the lesson, Walter," said Ed, "it's done him a lot of good. It saved me about ten hours of explanation."

Mr. Williams laughed and nodded pleasantly and walked off to the clubhouse.

Tom Joyce and Matt and Pat and Scoop came up to them.

"Welcome to the group," said Matt, "the First Round Club."

"Yeah," said Scoop disgustedly. "Now Dan Slade'll get through the next few rounds easily. And I'll have to write about it."

"He won," said Tom, "so he deserves it."

"That's right," said Ed, "that boy plays real well."

"Win'll beat him in the Juniors," said Matt positively.

"Maybe," said Ed, "we'll see. There's plenty of time before that."

"I mean the Local Juniors," said Matt; "that's in a couple of weeks."

"Well, he's got some work to do before that," said Ed. "I'm going to work him real hard or Dan will beat him."

"No," said Matt.

"Yes," said Ed.

"All right, Matt, take it easy," said Win. "I'm very grateful for your confidence, but believe it or not, Ed knows what he's talking about."

"Oh I believe it all right," said Matt. "I'm just looking for revenge and it's a cinch *I'm* never going to beat him."

Ed slapped Win on the back. "You'd better start thinking of the doubles. You aren't all the way out of this tournament yet."

CHAPTER TEN

A Doubles Match

"You know," said Matt, as they walked to the court for their first doubles match, "if we can get through three rounds we'll probably play Dan Slade and his partner."

"I noticed that," said Dan. "Of course, he has to get through three rounds too."

"He will," said Matt. "I just want to make sure he doesn't get through the fourth."

Win grinned at his friend. "Okay," he said, "let's try and make sure he doesn't."

They were playing two men, weekend players, one of whom was a doctor and the other owned a drugstore in Dixboro. They greeted the two boys pleasantly and joked about the difference in ages between the two teams.

"Take it easy on us, fellows," said the doctor, "don't run us to death."

"That's right," said the druggist; "we just play this game for fun, so we can't be too good."

Win laughed. "We play it for fun too, sir," he said, "so that makes us even."

"I'm still groggy from my match with Dan Slade," said Matt. "I'll be lucky to be able to run at all."

"Ha," said the doctor, "at your age? I know you young lads. Five minutes after you say you're exhausted, you get up and play for another two hours."

They spun for service, the boys won and they went out on the court to warm up.

The two men had been telling the truth—they played for fun. They enjoyed themselves immensely, but they were no match for Win and Matt.

The boys hit the ball too hard and too accurately for their opponents, but it was mainly their youth that served them. They made some saves and gets that had the two men goggling in surprise.

The doctor didn't hit the ball hard, but he had a tricky little spin on his shots and he knew where to hit the ball, and so did the druggist. As a result, they had a lot of fun but it was over in about forty-five minutes.

They all came to the net to shake hands.

"Well, I told you," said the doctor, smiling at

them; "it was fun but there's no substitute for youth."

"Come on, Doctor," said the druggist, "these boys would have beaten us anyhow."

"Oh, I know it," said the doctor, "but let me salvage some pride."

They congratulated the boys and wished them luck, then left for the locker room.

Win and Matt went over to the officials' desk to report the scores. Ed Partridge was sitting there. "Well?" he said.

"Two and three," said Win, meaning six–two and six–three.

"I watched some of it," said Ed. "Sit down here a minute."

They sat down in some lawn chairs.

Ed began drawing on a piece of paper. "Doubles is a game that is tactically much different from singles. I have known some great singles players that together couldn't beat two mediocre singles players playing well together. The reason is very simple. In doubles, what you do, where you are on the court, and how you place your shots—all change a lot from singles. With four men on the court, the position of the opponents is the most important thing." He finished his drawing and showed it to them, and as he talked he drew examples on the paper. "Now if, for example, you are at the net, where you generally should be in doubles, hitting a ball hard, unless it is an overhead smash, won't do you too much good because the shot itself is too difficult. But a nice easy angle between your opponents—" he drew a line on the paper—"will be completely out of their reach." He continued for almost half an hour, stressing the importance of position and placement. "Also, rush the net after every serve. Don't get caught one up and one back for more than one shot if you can help it; and if you are both at the net, your chances are that much better." He put down the pencil and smiled at them. "Any questions?"

"It looks easy," said Matt, studying the diagram, "but I'm willing to bet it isn't."

"Nothing that's acquired is easy," said Ed; "there are too many unexpected possibilities. One of which is your opponents. They're going to be trying the same things on you, remember."

"Whom do we play next?" asked Win.

"In about fifteen minutes," said Ed, "you play two more old duffers. Old in comparison to you two. One of them is almost sixty but the other one is only about thirty-two. They are father and son, and they know what they're doing. It's Hunter Davis and his son Evan. They've played a lot of tennis in their day."

"I know about Evan," said Win; "he used to be quite a good athlete here at Dixboro High. I haven't seen him for years."

"Well, his father taught him," said Ed, "and Mr. Davis, when it comes to tactics, is an expert."

"Isn't Evan Davis a writer or something?" asked Matt.

Ed grinned. "Yes, quite a good one I understand. He has a beard too, but that won't affect his tennis."

"Well," said Win, "we might as well go over."

"If you beat them," said Ed, looking at them with a glint of amusement on his face, "you'll probably play Dan Slade and his partner."

"We know," said Matt grimly, "we know."

The Davises, father and son, were waiting for them on the court.

Mr. Davis was a medium-sized, stocky man, deeply tanned, with a crown of pure-white hair. He certainly didn't look sixty years old; he was not in the least overweight, and his legs in his white tennis shorts were brown and well-muscled.

His son was something to see. He was taller than his father, almost completely bald, and with a full beard and mustache. He was even more tanned than his father, his bald head was almost black from the sun. He was immaculately dressed, wearing a dark-blue blazer with a heavy corded emblem on the breast pocket. He evidently knew what a sight he presented because he grinned at Win and Matt, showing strong, white teeth.

"Don't let it frighten you, boys," he said, "it's human."

Win flushed a little in embarrassment. He had been staring and so had Matt.

"He's a good partner," said Mr. Davis. "Everybody's so busy watching him, that their tennis suffers."

When they started warming up, it was easy to see what he meant. Evan Davis on a tennis court was a riot, and evidently a lot of people knew it, because the stands near the court were starting to fill up and they were all watching him.

First of all it was apparent to Win that Evan was a very good player. He had the big game, and when he was hitting to Win at the net during the warm-up rally, he hit the ball so hard that Win could barely react in time to volley it back. He bounded around the court with great energy and he talked constantly—to Win, to Matt, to his father (who didn't listen), and most of all to his friends in the stands. When he missed one, or hit into the net, he would shout loudly in one foreign language or another. He started hitting lobs to Win and he hit one so high that the ball almost went out of sight. The crowd laughed and applauded but Win noticed that the ball came down right where it was supposed to. Twice he hit the ball left-handed rather than step over for it. Tennis is generally considered a quiet, polite game —there is a very strong form and etiquette for it, but Evan Davis was completely unconcerned about that. He played with great enthusiasm and he continually tried for the hardest shot, quite contrary to the tactics that Ed had taught Win.

His father couldn't have been more different. He didn't hit the ball very hard but he hit with great accuracy. He anticipated shots easily and, in spite of his age, was very quick at the net. But the crowd had gathered to watch Evan, and he was giving them quite a show.

The Davises won the serve, and Evan served first. He threw up the first ball and hit it with tremendous force. The ball hit the tape at the top of the net with a terrific smack and bounced at an angle all the way into the stands. Evan stared at the net, then walked up to it and carefully measured it with his racket. Of course it was exactly the right height. He glared at it again, then went back to serve. The crowd was delighted and laughed with pleasure.

His second serve was cut so hard that when it just cleared the net it almost bounced back over and Matt, trying to reach it, flubbed it completely.

Matt walked over to Win. "Gee, Win, what are we going to do with that serve?"

"I don't know," said Win, "we'll just have to figure it out."

They didn't have to. Evan served doubles to Win and again to Matt. For the final points he didn't try his weird serve again.

It was a good match all the way. Matt was much better in doubles than in singles; his reactions were those of the natural athlete and both he and Win played very well. The difference was Mr. Davis.

His placements and lobs, his incredible steadiness from the back court, were hard to believe from a man his age. He seldom gave Win or Matt an easy shot to hit, and his net play was something to see. If either Matt or Win was even slightly out of position, if there was only about two or three inches of space left open, Mr. Davis would drop the ball right into that spot.

Evan Davis made some impossible shots, big Forest Hills kind of shots, but he also missed some important ones. Not content just to keep the ball in play, he tried time and again for tremendous placements straight down the outside line where the margin for error was very small. But he kept the crowd interested with his big play and his antics on the court. He didn't seem to care if he won or not, but he did seem to care about having a good time, and if that was true he was a great success. There was no question in Win's mind that Evan was a fine athlete; not only his great shots, but some of his returns bordered on the miraculous. Once he went back at top speed for a lob, and without turning around and still running as fast as he could, he made a negligent sweep of his racket and hit a high arching lob that came down like a mortar shell right on the base line. The ball bounced so high that Matt barely reached it and he hit it into the net despite his best effort.

Another time, Mr. Davis, trying to return a hard serve by Matt, hit a weak lob right to Win at the net. Win, who hadn't had many chances that easy, hit it with all his might, a smashing overhead right at Evan who was also at the net only about ten feet away. Somehow he got his racket on it, and the ball popped just over the net out of Win's reach. It was an extraordinary shot, part luck and part reflexes, but the crowd burst into applause.

Evan faced them and made a deep bow, then turned to Win and, pulling a white handkerchief from his pocket, waved it at him.

"I surrender, Hadley," he cried; "I give up!"

The crowd loved it.

Usually anyone who played with the noise and flamboyance of Evan Davis would have annoyed Win, but it was impossible to get angry at the man. He was prompt and sincere in his praise when Win or Matt made a good shot, and he was absolutely honest on his calls of questionable points. Twice he reversed the umpire's call of out and gave the point to the boys. Both times Win had been in a position to see the point and Evan was unquestionably correct. He never argued about a point, accepting all the calls against him.

Win noticed also that he covered a lot of ground that would ordinarily have been his partner's. It was clear that he was trying to save his father from running as much as possible. The result was that he was all over the court himself.

His father was evidently used to him and his method of playing and Win could see that they were very fond of each other. They were constantly grinning at each other on a good play, and often Evan would pat his father on the back after a point.

He made too many mistakes in his attempts to make the big shot but—one thing—he never was out of position. His father had evidently trained him well on that score. The two of them covered the court like a blanket and, slowly, they began to forge ahead in the match. They won the first set six–four and were leading three–one in the second when it happened.

Win hit a freak shot; it hit the net and took a high, lazy bounce at an abrupt angle away from the court. Evan had been playing at the net but on the other side. He took off immediately, dashing with all his speed to reach the high-bouncing ball. Lying off the court about twenty feet from the outside line was a big roller used for rolling the clay courts. Evan, with his eye on the ball, didn't even slow down.

"Watch out!" shouted Win and Mr. Davis in unison.

Evan hit the ball back, a high arching lob, and the next moment he ran full tilt into the roller. It caught him at the knees and he flipped into the air. He turned a complete somersault, ducked his head and did a beautifully co-ordinated gymnast roll, coming up on his feet. He had dropped his racket but he grabbed it from the ground and tried to get back to the court to continue play. As he put his weight on his right leg, he winced and fell.

Win leaped the net and ran to him, as did the others.

"Are you all right?" asked his father anxiously.

"I'll make it," said Evan, trying to grin. "Just give me a bullet to bite on."

"Oh, oh," said Matt, "you're bleeding."

"I cut my leg on something," said Evan.

On the calf of his right leg was a long, jagged gash, and the blood was flowing from it freely.

By this time several officials had gathered, one with a first-aid kit. He looked at the cut. "I don't think it's serious," he said; "no need for stitches. I think I can bandage it."

"It's all right," said Evan, "but I pulled a muscle in the leg too." He smiled up at his father. "That's it, I guess. I don't think I'll be able to walk on this for a couple of days, let alone run on it." He smiled again. "At least I got the point."

"It's my fault," said Ed. "I should have made sure that that roller was farther back."

"It's nobody's fault," said Mr. Davis. "It's just one of those things."

"Are you sure you can't play?" asked Win.

"Maybe if we waited awhile. Or we could play it off tomorrow."

"That's very kind of you, son," said Evan, "but I won't be playing on this leg for a week or two." He was helped to his feet and he gingerly put his weight on the leg. "No. That's all for a while."

"We forfeit," said Mr. Davis and held out his hand to Win. "I don't mind forfeiting to you two boys one bit."

"Gee," said Matt, "I hate to win it that way."

"Me too," said Win. "Are you sure you can't play?"

"I'm sure," said Evan. "We couldn't lose to two nicer fellows."

"You wouldn't have lost," said Win.

Evan grinned. "You never know, Hadley."

Matt and Win helped him off the court and into the locker room. They shook hands again, and the two Davises wished them luck.

Ed was waiting for them at the officials' table.

"That was my fault," he said, "no matter what Evan says. I run this tournament and I should have known that a madman like Evan would find a way to run into that roller."

"He's a terrific player," said Win, "and so's his father."

"He *could* be," said Ed, "but he isn't because he plays strictly for the fun of it; he doesn't care if he wins or loses. You could beat him."

"I could?"

"Easily. But when he plays doubles with his father, they're a real threat to anybody around here. They play the game the way it should be played as far as tactics are concerned. I hope you two learned something from Mr. Davis."

"I'll say," said Matt. "He always seems to find the spot where I'm not."

"Headwork," said Ed, "and great control. His son has twice the shots, but always tries for the big one. You can't make them often enough in this game."

"Now what?" asked Win.

"You win," said Ed, "and tomorrow it's you know who."

"He won?"

"He and his partner won," said Ed. "It takes two to win in doubles."

"Tommy DeCenso, huh?" said Matt.

"A good little player," said Ed; "his father taught him too."

Mr. DeCenso was the pro at the country club, and Dan Slade's teacher and Tommy DeCenso's father.

"What time?"

"One o'clock. And remember. If you paid any attention to the way the Davises played you should have learned something. They weren't caught out of position more than twice and that was only because Mr. Davis can't run the way he used to."

"I should run that way now," said Matt.

CHAPTER ELEVEN

Another Doubles

THE NEXT DAY at one o'clock was not the best time for a tennis match. Dark clouds hung low, the wind was gusty with the smell of rain. Off in the distance lightning flashed, and one could hear the faraway boom of summer thunder.

"Better get started," said Ed, looking worriedly up at the sky.

"Sooner the better," said Dan Slade. "I want to get this over with. I have better things to do."

"Why don't you run along and do them, then," said Matt.

"All right," said Ed firmly, "you boys are here to play tennis. So get going before we get flooded out."

They warmed up quickly. Dan Slade and Tommy DeCenso won the toss and Dan elected to start serving. He aced Matt on the first serve and a small grin appeared on his face. He continued serving and won the game at love. Win and Matt didn't get a point. As they changed courts, Dan said to Matt, "This won't take long, I see."

"That's right," snapped Matt. "We'll see, all right!"

"Come on," said Win as they walked to their side of the court, "he's just trying to get your goat. If he does, you'll play worse."

"Well, if he's trying, he's doing a good job," said Matt, his face set in grim lines.

"Pay attention," said Win, "never mind him."

Win won his serve, and Tommy DeCenso was just beginning his when the rain came.

The rain came suddenly and heavily. The players ran for their sweaters and racket covers and the umpire climbed hastily down from his chair. They all ran to the clubhouse.

"What do you think, Ed?" asked Win, watching the heavy drops splash on the clay.

"Depends," said Ed. "These courts drain real well. If it doesn't rain more than five minutes, they'll be dry in another ten. If it rains this hard for ten minutes, we'll have to play it off tomorrow."

"I hope it stops," said Dan. "We can finish this in about twenty minutes, then I won't be late for my date."

"If your date is in another hour," said Matt, "you'd better plan on being late."

"Why?" asked Dan innocently.

"You know why, Slade," said Matt. "Because we're going to beat your ears off!"

"Say," said Tommy DeCenso, puzzled, "what is all this?"

"Nothing," said Win; "just a couple of little kids making noise."

"I'll make noise all right," said Dan, "on the court."

"What's wrong with these guys?" asked De-Censo. "Sounds like some kind of grudge."

"All right," said Ed Partridge, "if you guys want to argue or scrap, do it somewhere else. Here we play tennis and that's all. Get me?" He looked at each boy in turn. Nobody said anything.

"It's stopping," said Win finally, and they all looked up at the sky. The wind was blowing the heavy clouds away, and off to the north bright blue sky was showing through the overcast. The rain stopped as suddenly as it had come.

"Okay," said Ed, "give it a few minutes, then try it again. It should be dry enough by then."

It was. The sky cleared and the sun shone down brightly. The game continued in earnest.

It was a close match, standing at four–five. As they changed courts, Matt couldn't resist saying, "Looks like your big date will have to wait."

"Oh, she'll wait," said Dan airily, as if he couldn't care less. "She's crazy about me."

"Who'd be nuts enough to go for you, Slade?" asked Matt.

"I thought you'd never ask, Hughes," said Dan, grinning at him. "Her name is Pat Hughes, and she'll wait."

"Why you—" said Matt, and started after him. Win grabbed him and held him back. "Matt!" he snapped. "Cut it out!"

"You heard what he said," said Matt, straining against Win.

"He said he had a date with your sister," said Win. "Relax. There's no law against that. Now simmer down."

"It's not true," said Matt; "he's a liar!"

Dan had been watching with amusement, but when Matt said that, he dropped his racket and walked up to him.

"Let him go, Hadley," he said. "Nobody calls me a liar!"

"You're a liar!" said Matt again.

Ed Partridge rushed out onto the court. He stood between the two of them and he was really angry.

"Now listen to me," he said. "If there is any more of this nonsense, any more at all, I'll disqualify both of you!" He looked at them with disgust. "What are you two, children? I don't care how you feel about each other, I don't care one bit. But I'm in charge here, I'm running this tournament, and I'm telling you for the last time if you two babies can't behave, you're out, and out quick! I'm not kidding, not in the least. If you two want to fight do it somewhere else, or out you go."

"He called me a liar!" said Dan. "I don't take that from—"

"You are a liar!" said Matt, anger in his voice.

"All right," said Ed. "You are both disqualified."

That stopped them. They looked at Ed in astonishment.

"I don't believe you boys understood what I was telling you," said Ed. "I run this thing, and I don't put up with babies. This is a senior tournament, not a nursery school."

"Wait a minute, Ed," said Win. "I promise you I'll keep Matt under control. There won't be any more of this."

"That's right," said Ed. "There certainly won't. Out!" he repeated.

"Mr. Partridge," said Tommy DeCenso, "I don't know what any of this is about, but if Win can keep Matt quiet I'll try to keep Dan quiet. I worked hard in this tournament, sir, and I want to play until I'm put out."

"Do you think you can do it?" asked Ed.

Tommy looked at Dan, and there was plenty of

meaning in it. "I'll do it," he said; "you can count on it."

"Win?"

"Believe me," said Win, "if Matt makes a peep, I'll fight him myself."

Ed studied them all for several moments. "All right," he said abruptly, "but this is it. No more or that's the end. And if you don't believe me, try me." He looked at them again, his anger still very apparent, then he turned and walked away. There was a silence.

"Gentlemen?" said the umpire pleasantly. He had been watching and listening with the greatest interest. "If you don't mind, shall we get on with the match?"

"Right away, sir," said Win and drew Matt away. "Look, Matt, I don't blame you for being mad, but you've got to forget it. He was trying to get you mad and he sure did it."

"Win," said Matt, "he sure did. I *am* mad. And I'm going to beat that guy if it's the last thing I do!"

"Calm down," said Win; "you can't play when you're mad."

"I can't, huh?" said Matt. "You just watch."

But Win was right. From that point on, Matt's playing got steadily worse. He tried too hard, he tried for too many things. He constantly got in Win's way going after a ball that was Win's, and he overhit in his anger and began hitting them out. And as the score mounted in Dan's favor he got madder and madder until finally he was almost useless as a partner.

It was still a close match because Win dug down deep and played some very fine tennis. He had hoped that perhaps Dan was as mad as Matt and would lose his fine touch, but if he was he didn't play like it. In fact he played better, if anything.

Win and Matt lost in two sets, seven–five, six–four.

When the last point was lost, Matt turned to Win. "I'm not going up there to shake that guy's hand. I just won't."

Win looked at him and his face was cold. "Oh, yes, you will," he said. "They beat us and I think you know why. We're both going up there and do the right thing. Believe me, Matt."

Matt looked at him, startled. Then a sheepish grin broke out on his face. "Okay," he said, "but I won't like it."

"You don't have to like it," said Win, clapping him on the back; "you just have to do it."

They shook hands, Dan and Matt just touching briefly, then they walked off the court.

Tommy DeCenso came up to Win. "I don't know what it was all about, Win," he said, "but it ruined a good match."

"Forget it, Tommy," said Win, "you played well enough to win it anyhow."

"What's the matter with those guys anyway?" asked Tommy.

"They just don't get along," said Win.

"You can say that again," said Tommy. "Well, great game, Win."

"Thanks, you too."

Back in the clubhouse, Win couldn't see Matt anywhere, and for a moment he thought he had gone after Dan Slade. Then he saw Dan on the other side of the big room, and a moment later Matt walked in and flopped down on the bench, a look of disgust on his face.

"How about that!" he said unhappily.

"How about what?"

"I just called home. Do you know that my sister really has a date with that crumb?"

Win chuckled. "Oh well," he said, "it's a free country."

Matt looked across the room at Dan. "Sometimes I wish it weren't—maybe I'd stand that guy up against the wall."

"You don't mean that," said Win.

"How do you know so much what I mean and what I don't?" asked Matt in an aggrieved tone.

"Because I know you, sonny," said Win.

Matt sighed. "I don't know what I'd do without you, I really don't. Next thing you'll start feeding me."

"You probably need help at it at that," said Win.

Matt started to answer, then stopped. He thought for a moment. "I'm sorry, Win," he said finally.

"That's all right," said Win, not pretending to misunderstand.

"No, it isn't," said Matt. "I lost it for us when I got so mad."

"We might have lost anyhow," said Win.

"Maybe," said Matt, "but I doubt it. The worst part was acting like that in front of Ed Partridge and the umpire. Ed was right when he called us babies."

"Kootchy koo," said Win, tickling Matt under the chin, "ums take ums shower now? Then ums take nice little nappy bye?"

"I'll kootchy koo you," said Matt, and chased Win into the shower room.

Dan Slade, standing alone in front of his locker, watched them go, a withdrawn, wistful look on his handsome face.

In the shower, Matt said to Win, "Now you've just got to beat Dan in the Local Juniors. That's in a couple of weeks, so get prepared."

"Don't worry," said Win, "I'll be ready. I think Dan needs to be beaten once in a while."

CHAPTER TWELVE

An Interlude

WHEN ED said that he would work Win hard on the more subtle shots of tennis, he certainly meant it. Every day after the courts had been rolled and marked, Ed would take Win over to the far court and go over and over the same shots. He had Win lob for three afternoons straight, nothing but lobs from every part of the court. Then he switched and had Win rush the net on every shot and volley Ed's return. Volley, volley, volley, for day after day until Win was getting the impression that it was illegal to take the ball on the bounce. Volleying, of course, was hitting the ball before it bounced, one of the most difficult shots in the game of tennis, and Ed was going to make sure that Win was good at it.

Win would get home at night exhausted. After supper, he would generally play one or two games of croquet with Matt and Scoop and Walt but he never stayed up late. He was too tired. He went to

bed soon after it got dark and got up early to
work on the courts. He enjoyed it thoroughly in
spite of the constant practice. He loved the game
of tennis—it was such an individual sport. If you
lost you couldn't blame anybody but yourself.

On an occasional Sunday, he would go for a
short cruise on Scoop's sloop, and then on Monday he went back to work with enthusiasm.

One day Ed stopped in the middle of the practice session and came to the net.

"You're getting too good for me," he said. "I'm
going to have to find someone who can get the ball
by you. Can you practice after supper instead of in
the afternoon? You could quit here early."

"Sure," said Win, "I guess so."

"Okay, starting tomorrow come back about
seven. There's still two hours of good light then."

"Whom are you going to get?" asked Win.

"I'm not sure," said Ed, "but I'll get somebody.
Just be here."

"I'll be here," promised Win.

He was waiting with Ed the next evening but
Ed refused to tell Win who was coming to rally
with him. "You'll see," is all he said.

A few minutes after seven, a large black car
stopped by the clubhouse and a tall, slim, handsome man in tennis clothes got out.

Win stared. "Walter Williams!" he said.

Ed chuckled. "Is he good enough for you?"

"Wow," said Win. "He's *too* good."

"He'll be a lot of help. This should be very valuable for you."

Walter Williams strolled up to them. "Hello, Ed. Mr. Hadley, how are you?"

"I'm fine, sir," said Win. "This is certainly very kind of you."

"The pleasure is mine," said Mr. Williams. "I haven't had any good tennis since we last played." He turned to Ed. "Volleying? Lobs? Position?"

"All of them," said Ed, "and work him to a frazzle."

"I'll do my best," said Mr. Williams. He picked up his racket. "Ready, Mr. Hadley?"

"Ready, sir."

It was the most rewarding workout Win had ever had. With Ed standing near him and telling him what to do, and Mr. Williams putting the ball exactly where he wanted it, Win began to understand the world of big competitive tennis.

They worked the whole week before the Local Juniors, and by the time Ed called it quits, Win knew more about the inner workings of a fine tennis player's mind and instincts than he had ever known before.

"All right," said Ed on the last Friday before the tournament, "that's enough."

"I have an idea, Ed," said Mr. Williams, "although I'll probably regret it. Why don't Mr. Hadley and I play a set? We've just been rallying up to now. Let's see what he's learned."

"It's all right with me," said Ed, "if you're not too tired."

"Playing with this lad has put me back in shape," said Mr. Williams—whom Ed had never seen out of shape. "How about it, Mr. Hadley?"

"I'd love to," said Win.

During the set, Win had to use everything he had learned plus all his natural talents to keep even with Mr. Williams. During the course of the set he also discovered that there were some things that he had yet to learn, as Mr. Williams outsmarted him again and again.

But Win was at the top of his form, his timing was perfect and he played better than he ever had. With the games at fifteen all, Mr. Williams held up his racket. "Enough. I'm running out of gas."

They went over and sat down with Ed.

"I think you've done it, Ed," said Mr. Williams. "I think you've got yourself a real winner here."

Win flushed with pleasure.

"He did pretty well," said Ed. "Not bad at all."

Mr. Williams laughed. "Come on, Ed, he did better than that, and you know it."

"All right," said Ed grudgingly, "a little better."

"That's a compliment, son," said Mr. Williams, "coming from Ed."

"I know it," said Win.

"I don't know how you do it, Walter," said Ed. "You still have that great game and you're in splendid condition."

"Oh, it's all right," said Mr. Williams, "but I'm not what I used to be."

"I looked you up in the Tennis Encyclopedia," said Win. "You won a lot of tournaments."

"Not the big ones though," said Mr. Williams, "although I did come close."

"Don Budge put you out at Forest Hills," said Win. "Was he as good as they say he was?"

"He was that," said Mr. Williams. "He was great."

"What was it like?" asked Win. "Playing in all those big tournaments?"

Mr. Williams thought for several moments. "It was the greatest part of my life," he said finally. "There's nothing like it. Wimbledon in the early summer is my favorite, but Rome and Paris in the spring are pretty nice too. I played the amateur circuit for two years, then went to law school. I never regretted it, of course, you can't play tournament tennis all your life; but now and then I miss it." He was lost in thought for a while. "Of course, a lot of people think sports are silly, grown men playing games, putting great importance on them. But so many good men have done it, so many good men still do it, there must be more to it than just hitting a little white ball over a net. I got a lot out of it, and I'm still getting a lot out of it. I wouldn't have missed it for anything."

There was silence for a while, then Win asked, "Do you think maybe I could ever do it?"

"Well," said Mr. Williams, "Ed probably wouldn't tell you this—he'd be afraid of spoiling you, but he knows and I know that you have all the equipment you need. All it takes is sticking with it."

"I'd love to have a crack at it," said Win. "It sounds exciting."

"It is," said Mr. Williams, "but it's work and dedication too—don't think for a moment it isn't."

"I don't," said Win, "Ed has made sure of that."

They all laughed and Ed looked pleased. It was getting dark when Mr. Williams stood up. "Well, I've got to go. Can I drop anyone?"

"Me," said Ed. "Thanks, Walter. My wife has the car."

"Mr. Hadley?"

"No, thank you," said Win. "I think I'll walk. I feel like it."

"It's good for the legs," said Mr. Williams, "and that's one of the differences between you and me now. I couldn't walk home now if my life depended on it. I'm too tired. You wore me out."

Win grinned at him. "I don't believe it for a moment, sir," he said, "but it's very kind of you to say so. And thank you for everything. I've learned a lot."

"All I ask," said Mr. Williams, "is that you make some use of it."

CHAPTER THIRTEEN

Scoop's Pink Bomb

"WELL," said Matt, "here's your first big chance." He held up the *Dixboro Advocate's* sports page. LOCAL JUNIOR FINAL FINDS HADLEY AND SLADE IN CENTER COURT, it said. The article had a byline by Scoop Slocum.

Win rolled over and squinted at it. "It's his big chance, too."

"You've got to beat him," said Matt.

"Why?" asked Win. "I don't have to beat anybody."

"You're joking!" Matt looked hurt. "Have you forgotten how he made a clown out of your bosom pal, your dear friend and compatriot, Matt (the Tiger) Hughes?"

"Well *you* beat him, then."

"I've tried," said Matt with mock sadness, "you saw what happened."

"I went out in the first round too," said Win.

"Yeah, but look who it took. Walter Williams, for Pete's sake."

Win laughed and sat up. "I'm just kidding. I'd

sure like to win it. It'll make a difference in the State Juniors, I'm sure."

"It sure will," said Matt. "If you beat him this time, he won't be so confident in the fall."

They were stretched out on the croquet lawn at the side of the Hadley house, waiting for Scoop. They were all going to the finals together.

"You know," said Matt, "Dan hasn't forgiven us yet about his boat. He still thinks we could have saved it. He never did find it. It must have sunk."

"That doesn't make sense," said Win, "it was all wood. It has to be somewhere unless it broke up."

"Well, he's still blaming us all over town," said Matt.

"Who's he told?" asked Win.

Matt laughed. "Me," he said; "after he beat me, he reminded me."

"You told me that," said Win, "but if you'll excuse me, you're not exactly everybody in town."

"All right, all right," said Matt, "I hope you beat him anyhow."

"Seriously," said Win, "so do I."

An old beat-up Ford, brightly painted a wild pink, wandered haphazardly up to the curb.

"Hey," shouted Scoop, "last bus to the Country Club."

Matt stood up. "Bus? Bus? That's a bus?"

"Only pink bus in town," said Scoop. "Isn't it beautiful?"

They walked over to the vivid jalopy.

"You're late," said Win. "Do you want me to forfeit?"

"Sorry," said Scoop, "but we'll make it. Lots of excitement down at the paper today. A couple of guys held up the bank in Crawford last night. You know they're open late Fridays." He scrutinized Win and Matt searchingly. "What were you two doing last night?"

Matt's eyes narrowed. "We was over to Crawford," he growled; "we had some business at the bank. Money business."

"Yeah," snapped Win, falling in with it, "what's it to ya, fella?"

Scoop began to shake violently in every limb, and he covered his face with his hands. "Don't, fellows," he begged. "I won't squeal. Just don't work me over. I can't stand pain. It hurts."

"Ya don't know the half of it," snarled Win.

"Please, fellows!"

"Whaddaya think," said Matt; "shall we work him over a little, shake him up like?"

"Aw, I don't know," said Win, "he's such a puny little thing. Let's throw him back and forget about him."

"Okay," said Matt, "but maybe just one little punch right on the button?"

"Please, please, I won't squeal!"

"See you don't," snapped Matt.

"Come on," said Win, "enough's enough. The hero has to go into battle. I'll be late."

They piled into the pink horror and it rocked violently.

"Maybe I'd better take a cab," said Win, "this might never make it."

Scoop was hurt. "Are you kidding? This bus always makes it." He accelerated and there was a series of sharp explosions.

"Holy cow!" said Matt. "I think those bank bandits are after us!"

"Relax, son," said Scoop complacently, "you might call that a sort of warning to other drivers."

"Well, they sure need it," said Win. "Slow down. I'd rather be late than a handsome corpse."

"I repeat, boy tennis hero, relax. You couldn't be in better hands."

"Well, if that's true, we're in real trouble," said Matt. It was a prophetic remark.

When Scoop turned off the main road, Win said, "Hey, where are you going?"

"We'll take the short cut," said Scoop, "out past Jones's farm."

"Well," said Win, "it's shorter, but it's a terrible road."

"That's all right," said Matt, "it's a terrible car—so we're even."

They were about three miles away from town on the back road to the country club, which was well on the outskirts of Dixboro, when the bright-pink jalopy's motor suddenly developed an advanced case of the hiccups. It puffed and clanked and then, all at once, it just gave up. They coasted to the side of the road and got out.

"Holy cow," said Win, "what's wrong?"

Scoop threw up the hood and peered inside. "Gosh, Win, I don't know. It never did this before."

"Great," said Matt. "I'll tell you what's wrong. You threw a rod."

"I think you're right," said Scoop disconsolately. He straightened up and turned to Win. "Gosh, Win, I'm sorry. How are you going to get there on time?"

"I don't know," said Win, looking down the deserted road. He patted Scoop on the shoulder. "Take it easy," he said, "I know you didn't plan it."

"Well, now what?" said Matt. "With a thrown rod this heap isn't going anywhere."

"We have to figure out something," said Win. "If I don't get there pretty soon, I'll forfeit the match to Dan."

"It's at least three miles," said Scoop. "Can you trot it in time?"

"I doubt it," said Win; "and if I did I'd be too tired to play when I got there." He looked up and down the road again. "Maybe somebody'll come along."

They all looked for a sign of a car. There was nothing.

"Where's the nearest house?" asked Scoop.

"Maybe we could get somebody to drive us over."

"Well, Jones's is about a mile and a half," said Matt, "but if you'll pardon my mentioning it, the Slades' house is closer."

"Oh, great!" said Scoop. "That would be just peachy—asking one of the Slades to take Win to the club so he could beat their son."

"They won't be there anyhow," said Win; "they'll all be at the country club."

"What about their hundreds of servants?" asked Matt. "Maybe we could get the butler or the upstairs maid to drive us."

"Oh, knock it off," said Win, "this isn't funny."

"Hey!" said Scoop suddenly. "Here comes a car!"

They all spun around and saw a shiny convertible coming down the road.

"I don't believe it," said Matt; "it couldn't be, it just couldn't."

"Holy mackerel," said Scoop. "Talk about poetic justice!"

The sleek car slid to a stop and Dan Slade looked out at them.

"Yes?" he said. "Something I can do?"

"You'd better hurry, Slade," said Matt, "you'll be late."

Dan smiled. "That's true, Hughes, I'd better go."

"Hey, wait a minute," said Scoop, alarmed. "Give us a lift to the country club. I threw a rod."

"That's understandable," said Dan calmly, looking with scorn at the pink jalopy.

"Well, come on," said Scoop, "aren't you going to give us a lift?"

"I'll give Win a lift," said Dan, looking at him coolly. "He's the only one that has to be there."

"Don't be silly, Dan," said Win. "I won't go without them."

"Wait a minute," said Scoop. "Let me get this straight. You mean you'll take Win but not us?"

"Correct."

Before anyone else could speak, Matt said, "If Win doesn't get there, you'll win by forfeit, Slade; I suppose you've thought of that."

Dan looked thoughtfully at Matt. "Do you think I'd do something like that?"

Matt was disgusted. "I sure do," he said.

"I guess you're right," said Dan. "I'm awfully glad you reminded me." He smiled very pleasantly, threw the big car suddenly into gear and, with a rip of the tires and the sound of scattering gravel, sped off down the road toward the country club.

The three stared after him, unable to believe their eyes.

"Can you believe it!" gasped Scoop. "He *did* go!"

"Why, that crumb!" said Matt. He turned to Win who was still looking down the road. "Well, Win, I guess that settles that!"

CHAPTER FOURTEEN

An Uneasy Victory

WIN STARED thoughtfully down the road at the disappearing car. "You know," he said slowly, "that really surprises me. I never for a minute thought Dan Slade would do something like that."

"Well he did," said Matt. "I always said the guy was a creep."

"I never went for him either," said Scoop, "but this is too much!"

"Now what?" asked Matt.

"Well," said Win, "we might as well start walking. I'll never get there in time anyhow. At least we can go and explain what happened."

"Man, I tell you when I see that crumb again, I'm going to go right up one side and down the other," declared Matt, "I mean it."

"Seriously—" said Scoop, and Matt interrupted.

"Don't you think I'm serious?" he asked, and he was truly angry.

"I don't mean that," said Scoop. "We've talked about Dan before and we've called him a crumb and a creep and all that. We were mad when he accused us of losing his boat when we probably saved his life. But this is downright nasty, trying to win a tournament like this. He could have picked us up."

"Yes," said Win, "he could have. But you two didn't make it too easy for him."

"Us? What did we do?" asked Matt.

"Up to now I would have suggested trying to be nice to the fellow," said Win, "but now I don't know. When he drove up we weren't too friendly. He didn't *have* to pick us up, you know."

Matt stopped walking and looked hard at Win. "Are you defending him?"

"No," said Win.

"I don't get you," went on Matt. "How come you never get mad at that guy? You're always sticking up for him, and what has he done to deserve it?"

"Well, he never did anything really crumby until right now," said Win. "The other stuff—at least I could understand a little of why he acted the way he did."

"But not now, huh?" asked Scoop.

"Not now," said Win, and his eyes narrowed a bit. "No, not now."

"Wait a minute!" Matt grabbed Win's arm and pointed. "Here comes another car! Maybe the driver'll take us to the club!" He looked happy for a moment. "And then you can beat Dan Slade's ears off!"

"He's heading the other way," said Win. "Maybe whoever it is won't want to turn back."

"He'll go," said Scoop. "I'll bring out all my biggest words and talk him into it."

They stood in the middle of the road, waving their arms madly, trying to make certain the car wouldn't pass without stopping. It didn't.

"Need a lift?"

"Ed!" gasped Win. "How did you know we were stuck out here?"

"Tom Joyce told me," said Ed. "Wait'll I turn the car around."

When they were all in and headed back, Win asked, "How did Tom Joyce know we were out here?"

"I don't know," said Ed. "He just came over and said you were stuck out on Jones Road, so I came out."

"Dan told him," said Win thoughtfully; "that's the only way he could have known."

"Well, can you beat that!" said Scoop. "That guy is absolutely nuts!"

"What happened?" asked Ed, and Win told him.

"So that's it," said Ed. "He came up to me and said you would be a little late but that he didn't mind waiting and he didn't want to take it by forfeit."

"I tell you," said Matt, "I'm going to keep away from that guy. I can't figure him out at all and he spends all his time aggravating me."

"He seems to be a strange kid," said Ed, "but to get to the point, strange kid or not, he's going to be tough to beat today, and you'd better forget this little fracas and start concentrating on the match."

"Gee," said Scoop, "with all the action, I almost forgot it. I hope you mop him up, Win, after all the trouble he's caused us today."

"That's the funny part," said Win. "He didn't cause us any trouble. He could have saved us some maybe, but he didn't make that miserable pink bomb of yours throw a rod."

"Talk, talk, talk," said Matt. "If you'll listen to me, you'll beat him, then leave him alone. He has a bad habit of bringing trouble with him."

"Okay," said Ed, "that's enough. I want this boy to start thinking about playing the match."

They let Win out at the club locker room and he rushed to change his clothes.

It was a beautiful day with little wind, perfect for tennis.

When Win came out, Dan was leaning negligently against the umpire's stand, waiting for him.

"I see you made it, Hadley," he said politely.

Win went up to him. "Listen, Dan, I think that was pretty small of you not to pick us up. I don't know what you had in mind, or why you did what you did—and I don't want to discuss it. I came here for tennis and I came here to win, so let's get on with it." He picked up the new balls and went out on the court without waiting for an answer.

Dan watched him go, a dull flush rising up into his face. He turned abruptly and went onto the court, as the umpire who had heard the remarks watched in surprise.

They rallied in silence, both of them hitting the ball low and hard. When the umpire asked them if they were ready, they both nodded but didn't say anything.

While it lasted it was quite a match. It was a match between two really talented, well-conditioned, well-coached juniors, both with the big game and both with an understanding of the tactics. But more than that, it was two young players who wanted to win so desperately they could taste it.

There were a lot of people in the stands and all of them seemed to have a favorite, as there was considerably more cheering than is normal at a tennis match. Several times the umpire had to caution them to be quiet during the play.

The first set was of a caliber of tennis seldom seen in Dixboro, hard, with a variety of shots well placed, and the big serve larded with the unpredictable American twist.

The crowd was pleased and excited and noisy, but the two players were playing with tremendous concentration and never once did they say anything to each other.

Ed and Tom Joyce sat together in the stands and they realized fully what they were watching. They knew the strained relations between the two players, the importance each put on the match, and although they were disturbed by the intensity of the play, they were thrilled by its excellence. When the first set stood at twelve all, Ed turned to Tom.

"What is this? The Battle of Bull Run?"

"I'm not sure I like it," said Tom; "they're taking it too seriously."

"But the play, Tom, it's exceptional!"

"It certainly is," said Tom. "I've never seen anything like it in the Dixboro Juniors in my life. It's almost like Forest Hills."

"If they keep this up," said Ed with a chuckle, "they'll both be there some day, that's for sure."

"It's too bad someone has to lose," said Tom.

He had just gotten the words out of his mouth when Dan, rushing swiftly to the net for a tantalizing drop shot, slipped and slid hard into the umpire's chair. He rolled over and dropped his racket and grabbed his right ankle in both hands.

There was a groan from the spectators when they saw that Dan might be hurt.

Win ran to the fallen player, all his animosity forgotten.

"Are you hurt, Dan?" he asked.

Dan looked up at him and there was no friend-liness in his face.

"No," he said, and got painfully to his feet. He bent over and picked up his racket and started out to the court. His ankle turned and down he went again, and a gasp of pain came from his lips.

"Mr. Hadley," said the umpire, "would you agree to a short rest in order to determine if Mr. Slade can continue?"

"Of course," said Win.

A big, heavy-set man with a red face and iron-gray hair came out of the stand and down to the court.

"How about it, Dan?" he asked. "You all right, son?"

"Sure, Dad," said Dan, and he got up again.

"That's my boy," said Mr. Slade. "Get in there; don't quit now."

"Don't worry," said Dan, "I'm not going to quit." He walked back on the court and it was apparent to Win that, although he seemed to walk all right, he was still in pain.

"Can you continue, Mr. Slade?" the umpire asked Dan.

"Of course he can," said Mr. Slade.

"I was asking your son," said the umpire firmly.

"Yes," said Dan.

"Go get 'em, boy," said Mr. Slade and left the court.

"You all right?" asked Win.

"Serve," said Dan shortly.

Win looked at him for a moment, then shrugged and went back to the service line.

That ended the match. Although Dan didn't limp or fall down or even complain, he was completely ineffective from that point on. He hit all the balls well that he could reach, but he didn't reach many.

Win became a little embarrassed. He didn't know quite what to do. Dan wouldn't go after his placements and it was nonsense to hit the ball right at him. If he did that it would cease to be a match.

The match ended fourteen–twelve, six–love, and Win was the Juniors Champion of Dixboro. He went to the net and Dan walked firmly to him and they shook hands.

"Bad luck," said Win, "about your ankle, I mean."

"My ankle is just fine, thank you," said Dan and walked away.

Win watched him go and saw his father come up to him and begin to talk animatedly, but Dan pushed by him and went into the locker room.

All Win's friends came over to congratulate him. Mrs. Hadley was there and she was thrilled at her son's victory and planted a big kiss on his cheek.

Ed came over. "Where's Dan?" he asked. "We

want to present the cups. He gets the runner-up cup."

"He went into the locker room," said Win.

Ed looked at him. "You played very well, son," he said.

"Thanks, Ed," said Win, "but something happened to him. I think it was his ankle."

"Nuts," said Matt, "he wasn't even limping."

"He knew he was going to lose," said Scoop happily; "he was just faking. I knew it, he's just a fake."

"What do you think, Win?" asked Tom Joyce.

Win shook his head. "I don't know. He said he was all right."

"Well, we'll give him his cup later," said Ed, "we can't keep the photographer waiting."

"Oh, dear," said Mrs. Hadley, "that doesn't seem fair to Dan."

"You're right," said Ed, and he turned to another committee member. "Will you go get him, Mr. Anderson?"

"I'll get him," said Win.

He didn't see Dan at first in the dim locker room, then he spotted him sitting over in a corner with his back to the door. Win walked over to him and looked down.

Dan had his shoe off and was staring at his ankle. He didn't seem to hear Win's approach. Win stared.

The ankle was an angry reddish blue and had

already swelled considerably beyond normal size.

"How the devil did you play on that?" asked Win, shocked.

Dan looked around. "I did play on it though, didn't I?" He sounded dull.

"Just a minute," said Win, "I'll be right back."

He went back to the court and took both Scoop and Matt by the arm.

"Hey, what's going on?" asked Matt in surprise.

"Be quiet," said Win, "and come with me." His tone was so serious that they both came along without protest. He took them into the locker room where Dan was sitting and pointed to the ankle.

"Holy cow!" said Matt.

"Exactly," said Win. "Now let's all apologize for what we said."

Dan lurched to his feet, standing gingerly on his sprained ankle. "What's the big idea?" he said angrily.

"Look at that ankle!" said Scoop, staring at it.

Dan put his foot behind the other one. "All right, get out of here!"

"Not yet," said Win. "Well, fellows?"

"I agree," said Matt. "I was wrong and I apologize."

"Me, too," said Scoop.

"What for?" asked Dan. "What's going on?"

"We all thought you were faking," said Matt, "but nobody could fake with that ankle."

"Well, I don't need your apologies," said Dan

coldly. "Just leave me alone if you don't mind."

"Come on out and get your cup," said Win, "you deserve it."

"You can have it," said Dan, "I don't want the thing." He tried to push past them. "I've got to shower, let me through."

Win stopped him. "Just a minute, Dan. You don't want our apologies and you don't like us. Okay. But you earned that cup the hard way and I'm going to see you accept it."

Dan stared at him. "How?"

"If I have to carry you," said Win, and there was no question that he meant it.

Dan studied him for several moments, then shrugged. "All right," he said finally, "I'm in no condition for a fight." He stopped for a moment, then continued. "I would have won the big cup, Hadley, don't think I wouldn't have. If it makes you feel any better to see me accept the second-place cup, okay. But I don't settle for second place, no Slade ever does. I'll see you again in the State Juniors; then it'll be different."

"Maybe," said Win, "I wouldn't be surprised. But right now we're all going out there and get our pictures in the paper and accept the cups because that's the way things are. Got me?"

All at once Dan grinned. "Got you," he said, and sat down to put his shoe back on.

"Leave it off," said Matt, "your foot's too swollen."

"Hughes," said Dan, "when I want your advice, I'll ask for it."

"Excuse me," said Matt with obvious irony, and he looked at Win and shrugged.

Dan struggled into his shoe and tied it loosely. He limped to the door, and it obviously hurt him. It was a wonder he could walk. He turned at the door and looked back at them.

"Coming, children?" he said and went out.

"Here we go again," said Matt, "we're just one big happy family—the three of us and Dan Slade."

"Well," said Scoop as they went out, "I'm no big gladiator like you two, but I've had sprained ankles and the one he's got is a beaut."

"It sure is," said Win. "No matter what else we think, Dan's got what it takes in the courage department."

"I would call it guts," said Matt, "but I'm the vulgar type."

"Call it what you like," said Win, "he's got it."

"Yeah," said Matt, "it hurts, but I'll have to admit it."

"So nothing's settled," said Scoop suddenly.

"What do you mean?" asked Matt.

"I know what he means," said Win. "We still don't know who's better, Dan or me."

"So it'll have to be the State, huh?" asked Scoop.

"If it's anywhere," said Win, "it'll have to be the State."

CHAPTER FIFTEEN

Dangerous Passengers

"THIS IS THE LIFE," said Matt, and lay back on the cushions in the cockpit. "Keep her steady, skipper, the mate wants to sleep."

Scoop snorted. "It's your watch in about ten minutes, mate, so it'll be a short sleep."

"Captain Bligh," said Matt; "no heart. Hang me from the yardarm and whip me to ribbons if you wish, but first let me sleep."

Win and Matt were on Scoop's trim white sloop heading downriver toward the ocean. It was the Sunday after the Dixboro Junior Finals, and they were going on an overnight cruise to the Wyandot River Estuary. They had food on board, the bunks were made up and they all felt peaceful and relaxed with nothing to do but take turns at the helm for several hours more.

The wind was light and fluky, so, to make time they were under power alone.

Scoop was at the helm, standing on the lazaret and holding on to the backstay, steering with his bare foot.

Win was sitting on the cabin top with his shirt off, in his swimming trunks, enjoying the hot mid-summer sun.

"Where'll we tie up tonight, Scoop?" asked Win.

"I don't know," said Scoop. "I thought we'd anchor in a little gunkhole I know that's nice and protected and eat our dinner. If we turn in early, we can get an early start in the morning and maybe take a quick trip out into the ocean."

"Sounds good," said Win. "I've got plenty of time; Ed gave me Monday off because I'm a big hero tennis player."

"Well, if the weather holds," said Scoop, "we'll take a run outside for a couple of hours and give our intrepid mate a real fright."

"Who, me?" Matt didn't even open his eyes. "I'm not sure what intrepid means, but if it's the opposite of chicken, I'm your man. Nothing scares me." He adjusted his position. "Unless it's lack of sleep."

"Your watch," said Scoop.

"You're kidding."

"Your watch. Hop to it. This is a taut ship. You either relieve the watch on time or over the side you go."

Matt sat up. "In that case, I'll relieve."

It was that kind of day. They were in no hurry, had no special idea where they were going, and they didn't particularly care. The weather was perfect, the galley cupboards were full, and they were on their way to wherever they arrived; they would go back when they were ready.

Just before dark, they found Scoop's little bay which he called a gunkhole, and just offshore and at low tide, they threw over their hook. Scoop was very careful to make sure it was set firmly in the bottom so they wouldn't drag during the night. They were about thirty feet offshore at low tide; in the morning at high tide they would be more than a hundred feet off.

Scoop fussed around the boat for another few minutes, securing everything and checking again lines that he had checked already. He was that kind of sailor, already an expert, leaving nothing to chance.

Matt made dinner and it was quite a spread. They had big slices of ham, mashed potatoes that Matt had prepared—smooth with no lumps, a fresh green salad, some canned peas, canned fruit, and big glasses of milk.

"What talent," said Scoop contentedly, his mouth full of ham and mashed potatoes. "You'll make some man a great wife."

"I agree," said Win. "This is your true calling, son. Pass the potatoes."

"All right, knock it off," said Matt, very pleased,

"or I'll make Win do all the cooking tomorrow."

"No, no, anything but that," pleaded Scoop.

"Right," said Win, "I can open a Coke but that's about it."

"I didn't know healthy high school tackles could make mashed potatoes," said Scoop. "The canned stuff I can understand, but these potatoes are the greatest."

"Oh, it's not too hard," said Matt airily; "all it takes is intelligence—which leaves certain parties pretty well out of it."

"Hmm," said Win, "I wonder whom he has in mind."

"I don't really care," said Scoop, his mouth still full, "as long as he keeps up the good work."

After the dinner Win displayed his talent and opened three Cokes. Before he came back up the hatch he turned on the radio, and they sat there in the rapidly fading light, listening to the music and watching the clear bright stars come out one by one. It was cooler now, and the night was clear and quiet. They sat without talking until it was quite dark.

"Well," said Scoop, "it's late enough to turn in. We'll get up early tomorrow and go through the cut into the ocean for an hour or two. With this weather it should be real nice."

"Wake me at about eleven," said Matt stretching luxuriously.

"I'll wake you at six-thirty with the rest of us,"

said Scoop sternly, "and I don't want to have to soak you with some nice fresh river water to get you up either."

"Son," said Matt, "I don't think you're big enough to talk to me that way."

"I don't have to be big," said Scoop, without concern, "I'm the skipper, and if I wanted to I could probably hang you for mutiny."

"Gosh," said Matt, "I never thought of that. Six-thirty it is."

They went below, and undressing to their undershorts, climbed into their bunks.

An almost absolute silence fell, broken only by the chuckle of water hitting the hull now and then. They fell asleep almost at once.

It was Win who heard it first. He sat up in his bunk and listened. It came again, the bump of something against the hull, and then, clearly, the pad of bare feet on the deck above.

He reached over and poked Scoop who came awake immediately.

"What?"

"Shh! Listen!"

There was no mistaking the sounds, there was somebody on deck, and as they listened, somebody else pulled himself over the gunwale. The boat listed a bit under his weight.

"Who's there?" Scoop said it firmly with a touch of anger in his voice. It startled Win who had not expected it. They got out of their bunks.

A shadow filled the hatch, and Scoop snapped on his big flash catching the person on his way down the ladder. It was a big man, soaking wet, with a crooked grin on his face. Behind him they could see another pair of bare feet.

"Put it out, sonny," said the man in a soft Southern accent; "just put her down and I'll handle it."

"Who are you?" asked Win. "What do you want?"

"Nosy little fella, ain't you?" The man chuckled and Win felt a touch of fear. It was a chuckle but there was no mirth whatsoever in it. Scoop must have felt the same way because his voice broke just a little.

"What do you want?" he said.

The man reached over and simply took the flashlight out of his hand. "Light up a light," he said, pleasantly enough. "Man can't see nothing down here."

"Listen," said Scoop.

"That's all, sonny, don't get me riled. I said light up a light and so you better light me up a light one time."

There was no mistaking the hard edge in his voice and Scoop reached up and turned on the galley light.

"Awright, Henry," said the man, "come on down here. The marines have landed." He snickered lightly.

Another man came down the ladder into the cabin. He was not as big as the first man and much less prepossessing. He had a long, thin face, with a patchy, skimpy mustache. He was going bald, and what lank wet hair he had was standing up straight. His nose had been broken more than once and was mashed against his face. He breathed with his mouth open, making a sibilant, unnerving sound.

The big man snickered again. "Ain't he a sight?" he said. "Henry like to scare you to death the first time you see the man. But don't worry, Henry ain't dangerous. Ain't killed more'n three-four men. Four, wasn't it, Henry?"

"Aw, Buford," said the skinny man in a skinny sort of voice, "I ain't never killed no one. What do you want to talk thataway for?"

"Henry's too modest," said the big man; "he's a real killer all right." He turned suddenly to Win who was listening in astonishment to this exchange. "What's your name, sonny?"

"Win," said Win without thinking.

"Mine's Buford like Henry says. I figger we ought to get introduced so we can be nice and chummy." He suddenly noticed Matt in his bunk, sleeping quietly. "What's the matter with that one, he dead or something?"

"He's asleep," said Scoop.

"Ain't that nice," said Buford, "to be able to

sleep like that. I ain't slept in a couple of days. Maybe someday I can sleep like that."

"I know who you are," said Scoop suddenly.

The big man's head came around at once and he looked hard at Scoop. "You do, sonny? Now just who are we?"

Scoop realized his mistake but it was too late. "I don't know, I thought . . ." his voice trailed off under the direct stare of the big man.

"I believe you do know at that," said Buford. "Ain't he a clever little fella, now."

"All right," said Win, "what do you want, anyhow?"

Buford studied him for a moment. "I might have to watch you, sonny, you look pretty near growed up." He reached casually into his shirt and brought out a revolver. "Now no nonsense, hear? Henry and me we don't want no nonsense at all." He waved the gun negligently. "Awright?"

Win and Scoop didn't answer. The sight of the gun was too sudden and the knowledge that this was a very serious situation was made instantly clear.

"I see you're getting the idea." The man looked around the cabin. "Now we was out there in the bushes and we seen you fellers eating up a real storm. Now in my country when a feller comes in tired and cold, the home folks fix him up a nice feed. How about it?"

Scoop stood up. "All right, get off this boat," he said angrily. "I know who you guys are, you're the crooks that held up the bank at Crawford. We don't have anything here you'd want, so just . . ."

That was as far as he got. The big man brought his arm around suddenly and knocked Scoop sprawling onto Matt's bunk.

"Hey," said Win, leaping to his feet.

"Set, sonny!" snapped the man and his voice cracked like a whip.

Matt sat up in his bunk. "All right, all right," he said, "I'll get up." He saw the scene in the cabin and he blinked several times.

"Hello, sonny," said Buford. "From what I heard out there in the brush, you're the cook. So get up and start cooking. We ain't eaten for a long, long time."

"Hey, what is this?" said Matt; then he saw the revolver.

"Do what they say, Matt," said Win in a steady voice. "Then maybe they'll leave."

"Well, well," said Buford, "you settling down, Win. You ain't so scared no more. You growing up mighty fast." He gestured with his revolver at Matt. "Start cooking, sonny."

"Nuts to you," said Matt, with surprising courage, "you wouldn't dare shoot, you . . ."

The noise of the hammer being drawn back was loud and clear in the cabin. Buford pointed the gun directly at Matt. "Maybe I would, and maybe I wouldn't. You want to find out which it is, sonny?"

"Come on, Matt," said Scoop, "it isn't worth it. All they want is some food."

"That's first," said the big man, "we'll see about later."

"Doesn't he ever say anything?" asked Win, indicating Henry.

"Not unless I ask him something," said Buford. "He's real steady that way. He breathes so darn hard I don't think I could stand his talking. Could I, Henry?"

"Naw, Buford," whined Henry.

Buford laughed. "See that? Ain't he a sight though?"

"After you eat, what are you going to do?" asked Win, and he was really curious.

"Now that's a good question, sonny," said Buford. "We'll have to think of something."

"It won't help," said Win, and he wasn't afraid any more.

The man looked at him. "What won't help?"

"They'll catch you sooner or later."

Buford leaned back on a bunk and looked for a moment at Win. "You know something, sonny? You're probably right. We never should have tried it. You know why? I'll tell you why, and believe me I thought it over. Because we're not smart enough. I ain't more than normal bright and Henry here's downright stupid." He didn't even glance at Henry. "I don't know," he went on, "one thing led to another and here we are on some kid's boat in the middle of some river I don't even know the name of."

"Why don't you give yourself up," asked Scoop, "if you feel that way?"

"I don't know," said the big man, "probably because I don't know how."

"What do you mean you don't know how?" said Scoop. "There's nothing to it."

"Shut up, sonny," said Buford, but he didn't sound angry; "you're out of your class here, you don't have any idea what I'm talking about." He looked around at the three friends. "You're nice kids, you got nice things, a boat even. A nice boat. You talk good too. You don't know anything about me, so just kindly shut up."

"Well," said Win, "I don't think . . ."

"I said shut up!" snapped the big man, and all at once he wasn't friendly any more. He turned to Matt. "Where's that food, buddy?"

"It'll be ready in a minute," said Matt, working.

"Snap it up."

"Buford?" said Henry in his thin, scared voice.

Buford turned slowly to Henry and the look he gave him was deadly. "Henry, don't say nothing to me. I know for a fact you ain't got nothing to say, you ain't never had anything to say, and it sure ain't likely you gonna start saying something now."

Henry blinked at him, then subsided.

A silence fell in the small cabin, only the sounds of Matt's cooking breaking it. Win was now quite concerned again. He had thought for a moment the man would be friendly but his mood had changed rapidly and Win didn't know what to do. He had never met any men like this and he had no idea what they might do.

"Okay," said Matt shortly, "here's your food." He handed them two plates.

Buford handed the revolver to Henry. "Me first, then you," he said. "If one of them moves an inch, make it number five."

He ate sloppily with his hands, shoving the food down his throat, using the paper plate as a funnel into his mouth. He was hungry, that was easy to see. He took the gun from Henry. "Okay, Henry, eat."

He sat there and watched the three boys steadily, his expression getting harsher and harsher. Now the only noise was Henry gobbling his food greedily.

Buford broke the silence suddenly. "How much food you got on this tub?" he asked.

"Enough for two days," said Scoop, "you can have it all."

A slight smile with no humor in it flickered

over Buford's face. "Thanks, sonny, that's nice of you." He gave Henry the gun again. "Keep it on 'em, Henry; I'm going up and take a look around. I'm gonna check the tactical situation." He chuckled. "Learnt that one in the Army from a lieutenant. A nice boy, the lieutenant, like you boys some." He thought for a moment. "Poor boy got hisself killed one day." He sighed deeply, then went up the ladder and out the hatch. He closed the hatch, shutting them in the small crowded cabin.

For a while, no one said anything, but the boys had had time to think, and it didn't take much for them to realize the gravity of their situation.

Win thought he might as well try to talk to Henry. The little skinny man with the mashed face didn't look too formidable.

"Henry," said Win, "you know you won't get away with anything, don't you?"

"Don't," whined Henry.

"Don't what?" Win didn't understand.

"Don't talk to me. Buford wouldn't like it."

"Are you afraid of Buford?" asked Scoop, trying to put sympathy into his voice.

"Yeah," Henry whined, "I am. I'm scared of everybody, but mostly of Buford."

"How can you hold up a bank if you're scared?" asked Scoop.

"Oh it's easy, then," said Henry. "Now I gotta

tell you to shut up or Buford'll get real riled up. An' I don't want that at all."

The hatch banged to and the big, dangerous-looking Buford came down the ladder, filling the cabin with his bulk and presence.

"What time is it?" he asked.

Scoop glanced at the clock hanging on the bulkhead. "Five-fifteen," he said

"That's about it," said Buford. "Daylight real soon." He chuckled again. "That's part of my tactical situation figuring." He looked around at the three friends. "Who owns this boat?"

"I do," said Scoop.

"Okay," said Buford, "here's what we're going to do. We're going to take a trip."

"A trip? Where?"

"Right up the river. I should've thought about a boat before. That's what I mean, I ain't more'n ordinary bright." He shook his head. "They ain't looking for us on no river. How far'll this tub go before you got to gas up?"

"Not too far," said Scoop; "we used half the fuel coming down here."

"Then we'll get some." He grinned at Scoop. "Ain't that simple though?" He looked around the cabin thoughtfully. "Now I got something to say to you fellers and I want you to listen real close." His tough, unshaven face tightened. "I want you boys to understand just what's happening to you.

I don't think you do yet. Henry 'n me, we running from the law. We running real hard and we don't want to get caught and we ain't gonna get caught neither, 'cause you fellers gonna help us. We ain't got a thing to lose, and because you are nice young fellers we don't want to hurt you none, but, sonny boys, we'll do it if we have to, don't think we won't, 'cause like I said we ain't got a thing to lose." He looked at them. "Understand?"

"Sure," said Matt, "you're crooks, that's easy to understand."

Buford looked at him for a moment without expression, then sighed. "You got to make it tough. Your kind always got to make it tough. Henry?"

"Buford?"

"Okay."

The gun leaped in Henry's hand, and with a dull chunk the slug tore through the planking right next to Matt's ear. He gasped and sat down, his face turning white.

"See," said Buford, "that help any?"

The shot was a shock to all of them. Up to now it had been some kind of adventure, dangerous, but still an adventure. It wasn't any more. They were caught by two men who were desperate, and for the first time they really believed their lives might be in danger.

"Awright, now," said Buford, and he sat down. "We leave at first light, and anything—I'll say that agin, anything—you fellers do is gonna cost you real dear. 'Nuff said, now we understand each other." He gestured at the radio direction finder. "Is that box a radio?"

"Yes," said Scoop, his voice cracking again from the tension.

Buford grinned at him. He was certainly a man to chuckle and grin, thought Win. "Take it easy, sonny," he said, "just turn it on."

It was now five-thirty and Scoop tuned the radio in to one of the local stations.

"Good morning, friends!" said a bright and cheery voice, "good, good morning! And it is one too. The temperature at five-thirty is sixty-six degrees, the humidity only a light twenty-seven percent, the winds north north west at five miles an hour. A beautiful, beautiful day! A day for being outside, for games and fishing and boating!"

"Yeah," said Buford, grinning, "that's right, boating."

"And now a brief message from Holden Wilks the friendly auto dealer, who wants to show *you* how *you* can save money by driving down . . ."

"Talky, ain't he?" said Buford.

"So remember," said the bright voice, "at Holden Wilks you can be *sure* you will get the best. The best product, the best service, the quickest, easiest financing. So come on in and let Holden Wilks, the Smiling Yankee, serve *you!*"

"Yankee," said Buford, and spat on Scoop's clean floorboards.

"And now the news," said the anonymous voice, and for the first time even the announcer sounded genuinely interested.

"One of the biggest manhunts in this area's history is still combing the countryside for two gunmen who held up the Crawford National Bank and escaped with twenty-five thousand dollars late Friday evening. Their car was discovered last night abandoned in a field near Latham's Landing on the Wyandot Estuary. Police are using bloodhounds, and an early arrest is expected. The two men have been tentatively identified by police as Buford Harris, age thirty-seven, six feet one inch tall, an ex-convict with a long record for assault and attempted robbery. The second member of the duo is Henry Smith, age thirty-five, height five feet three inches, weight about one hundred and twenty pounds. A distinguishing feature is a badly broken nose. This man is very dangerous. He is known to have killed at least two men in the last few years and has been on the FBI's Ten Most Wanted list for over a year."

The announcer's voice went on but now none of the boys was listening. They were staring in fascination at the little man with the mashed-in nose. He had killed two men! That little scared man had killed two men!

Buford saw their expressions and grinned again. "They say two but it's really four, ain't it, Henry?" he said.

"Now, Buford," said Henry, hanging his head, "what do you want to talk that way for?"

The announcer went on. "There are roadblocks out all over the county, bus and railroad terminals are under surveillance and Captain Logan of the State Patrol expects an arrest very soon."

"How far does this here river back up?" asked Buford.

"About two or three hundred miles," said Scoop.

"Ain't that nice. We'll go as far as we can then. How long will it take?"

"About three and a half days," said Scoop, "if we're lucky."

"Three and a half days!"

"We only average about five miles an hour," said Scoop, "and we can't run at night, too many hazards."

"That's all right," said Buford, "the longer the better. If we disappear for a few days it'll throw them off." He motioned to Henry. "Come on up on deck," he said, "I got a few things to say to you private." He looked at the boys. "I'm closing this cabin up, so don't try nothing." They went up the ladder and the hatch banged to.

After they left there was a short silence.

"Wow," said Matt, "this is serious!"

"It sure is," said Win. "We'll have to figure something out."

"No," said Scoop. "I admit I'm scared. Let's do what they say and maybe they won't hurt us."

"I'm scared too," said Win, "but I still think we ought to watch them carefully. Maybe we can catch them off guard."

"Yeah," said Matt, "maybe we could jump them when they're asleep or something."

"Just a minute," said Scoop. "Don't you remember what that radio announcer said? He said that that little Henry Smith had killed two men. Buford says it's four. What's the difference? He's a killer! I say it's not worth it to take any chances!"

Win considered. "You're probably right," he said finally. "If we co-operate there's no reason they should hurt us. But let's keep our eyes open anyhow."

"Don't worry," said Scoop, "I won't be able to sleep with that little sneaky Henry Smith on board my boat!"

CHAPTER SIXTEEN

A Strange Trip

IT WAS A STRANGE CREW indeed that took the little sloop back up the river. Buford was in complete charge, and he kept the three boys under constant surveillance. Even if they had wanted to try something it would have been impossible. He kept two of them above deck at all times, while he and Henry Smith and one of the boys stayed below in the cabin. He had found the binoculars and stood a constant watch, standing in the hatchway where he could not be seen too easily and studied every boat that passed very carefully.

They were traveling entirely under power from the little auxiliary. There was not enough wind to sail, so the sails were furled on their booms.

The boys could barely say anything to each other—it was virtually impossible to say anything that either Henry or Buford did not hear.

Win was sure of one thing. Buford had said in his thoughtful moment earlier that he didn't think they would get away because they weren't smart enough. Win by now was inclined to think that it was quite true. For example, the two of them had used their own names and had made no secret of the fact that they were the bank bandits. Win was sure that the boys would have found out in time that the two men were the objects of the manhunt, but they might have been fooled for a while at least. So Win felt that if they were going to do anything to save themselves or to aid in the capture of the two men, it would have to be something the men didn't understand. The boys would have to fool them somehow, but it would have to be something that would not make them suspicious. Win was sure that neither man was quite normal and Henry Smith acted as if he were actually a little unbalanced. Win thought the situation over carefully, and he suspected that Matt and Scoop were doing the same, but there didn't seem to be any action to take.

They stayed in the middle of the river, and no boat came close enough for any kind of signal; and with the two men watching so closely they couldn't have given one anyhow, unless it was a very obvious one.

Strangely, it was Buford who gave Win the idea for a signal that might be effective yet would be meaningless to the two men. Buford stuck his head out of the hatch and in his hand were the yachting flags that Scoop usually flew when he was under way.

"What are these for?" he asked.

Scoop who was at the helm said, "They're my burgee and ensign."

"I seen them other boats got flags up," said Buford, "how come we ain't got any?"

"I forgot," said Scoop. "It's been sort of a busy morning. Besides it doesn't make any real difference."

"If them other boats got them up, it makes a difference," said Buford. "I don't want to look no different from no other boat."

It was then that the idea struck Win. "We better put them up, Scoop," said Win.

Scoop stared at Win, and something in Win's face made him nod. "I guess you're right."

"That's the boy," said Buford. "I think we'll get along all right." He tossed the flags to Win. "Put 'em up," he said.

Win took them and, without hesitating, he put the Yacht Club burgee on the backstay at the stern. Scoop opened his mouth to say something and just as quickly closed it. He looked away from Win.

Win then took the ensign and fastened it to the flag halyard at the mainmast. This was the crucial time. He put himself between Buford and the flag while he fastened it, then ran it up quickly. Buford watched it catch the wind, then looked away at another boat.

"That's better," he said with satisfaction; "now we got flags like them other boats."

"That's right," said Win, and looked casually away from the ensign flying upside down. The gamble had worked and even if it hadn't he would just have changed it, explaining that he had simply made a mistake.

Scoop glanced up at it too, but with no show of interest. He knew very well that the ensign flying upside down meant distress. It was the easiest distress signal to fly and any boatman would recognize it. *I hope,* said Scoop to himself, *I hope they will*.

Somebody did right away, and it was almost the end of the trip right there.

A powerboat came dashing by upriver, then slowed suddenly. The man at the controls cupped his hands and shouted, "You all right?"

"Answer him!" snapped Buford, ducking down in the hatchway and swinging up his gun.

"Sure," said Win, certain that the jig was up. "We're all right."

The man stared at him disgustedly, started to say something, then pushed forward on his throttle and roared away.

Buford stuck his head out of the hatch. "What's he mean are we all right? What's going on here?"

"I don't know," said Scoop quickly. "I don't get it."

"He had a reason," said Buford, his face hard and mean. "How come he stopped?"

"I don't know," said Scoop. "Guys like that are always making fun of sailboats. They're so slow compared to powerboats."

"Yeah?" Buford glared at him. "You better be right, sonny; you hear?" He looked around him searching for other boats, but at the moment there were none. "You better be right," he repeated, and went down into the cabin and said something to Henry Smith.

Win and Scoop looked at each other in relief. That had been close. If every boatman did that, maybe the signal was not such a good idea after all. Win knew why the skipper of the powerboat had been disgusted. The burgee was flying from the wrong place too. He had undoubtedly thought they were some young kids who didn't know the rules and flew their flags any old way out of ignorance.

As they approached Dixboro on the way up-river, more boats began to appear and in some of them were people that the boys knew. It was probably going to be a dangerous situation; somebody was sure to notice the flags and come too close.

Win hated to speculate on what might happen.

But a strange thing happened. To Buford it wasn't strange, since he didn't know what was going on; but to Win and Scoop it seemed most unusual. Two high-school friends came by in an outboard and they just waved casually and went on. Another powerboat came by a little later, and in it was the owner of the boat yard, Mr. Lawson, an old sailor who in his day had sailed on the big fishing schooners off the Grand Banks. He went by at about ten knots a hundred yards away. He also waved but made no move to stop.

Scoop couldn't understand it. Mr. Lawson had taught him all he knew about sailing, and that was plenty. He looked over at Win and shrugged. To himself he thought, They didn't even see it! The big sailors and yachtsmen! Scoop was bitter. He was scared and under the threat of a gun from two desperate men. And nobody saw the distress signal flying from the mainmast, obvious for anyone to see.

"They'll never help us," thought Win disconsolately, "what'll we do now?" He answered himself. There *was* nothing more to do. They would just have to take their chances, and with the type of men that were holding them, their chances didn't look too good.

CHAPTER SEVENTEEN

Captain Logan Takes Charge

"Now let's get this straight," said Captain Logan. "Who saw them first?"

"I did," said a man with a yachting cap pushed back on his head. "I passed them about an hour ago and they had their ensign hanging upside down from the mainmast and their burgee in the wrong place too. I went up to help but they said they didn't need any. I thought they were just some kids that didn't know any better. Mr. Lawson told me differently."

"Yeah," said Mr. Lawson. "This feller here came in for some gas and told me about some sloop flying the flags all wrong and then he said it was the *Four Winds,* so I knew right off that was impossible."

"Why is that impossible?" asked Captain Logan, looking big and competent in his state trooper uniform.

" 'Cause that's young Slocum's boat, an' I taught

him myself. He wouldn't fly them flags wrong unless he had a reason."

"I see," said the captain thoughtfully. "That's when you went out to check."

"Well, first I sent out my youngest in the outboard. I was busy. He come back and told me he was sure he saw some man ducking down in the hatch. So I went out in the big powerboat, and there ain't no question about it, there's something wrong out there. That's when I called you."

"You could see the men?"

"Just one," said Mr. Lawson, "a feller standing low down in the hatch."

"All right," said the captain. "Now who are all *these* folks?"

"I called the boys' folks," said Mr. Lawson. "Figured they ought to know."

"Are they in any danger, Captain?" asked Mrs. Hadley. She was very nervous but trying not to show it.

The Slocums and the Hugheses were there too and they listened with some concern for the captain's answer.

"Well," he said, "if the situation is the way it looks, there's no use pretending there's no danger. One of those men is a psychopathic killer and the other isn't much better."

"How do you know who the men are?" asked Walt Hadley.

"One of the bank guards recognized them," said the captain. "They've been wanted for a long time. There's no question about it."

"What are you going to do?" asked Mr. Slocum, an older version of Scoop. "We're all pretty concerned."

"I understand that," said the captain. "First I'd like to ask Mr. Lawson here some questions. How about the *Four Winds?* When is she going to have to refuel?"

"Well—" Mr. Lawson ruminated a moment— "it depends on how long they been running. They left here yesterday full up heading for the Wyandot Estuary and now they're almost back. They'll have to refuel pretty soon if they're going to go much farther."

"All right," said Captain Logan. "How about food?"

"They had enough for two or three days, Captain," said Mrs. Hughes, "I packed most of it for them." Then, she couldn't help it, tears came into her eyes. "Captain, what *are* we going to do?"

"We'll do all we can," said the captain, "I can assure you of that. And all we can is quite a lot, if you'll excuse my saying so." He looked at the families for a moment. "I think the best idea is for all of you to go home. You can't help, and we'll keep in touch with you and let you know how things are going."

"Oh, I couldn't do that," said Mrs. Slocum, "I want to stay."

"Stay where?" asked the captain reasonably. "We don't know where they're going."

"He's right," said Mr. Slocum. "We'll all go home and the captain will phone us when he hears anything." He looked with meaning at the captain, "Won't you, Captain?"

"I promise," said Captain Logan, "the minute anything happens I'll let you know."

"Captain," said Mr. Hughes, "we're mighty fond of those boys."

"Believe me, sir, I know how you feel. If it'll help I'll tell you what I really think. I think they're going as far upriver as they can. Then they'll leave the boys and there'll be no damage done. There is a real danger, I'll tell you honestly. If the two men get suspicious, they are liable to do anything. They're desperate and using a boy as a hostage won't bother them for a minute. I probably shouldn't be telling you this but I want you to know the situation so that if you feel we're going too slowly on this thing you'll know why. We want to protect the boys in every way possible. We can't afford to let those men know we suspect anything. We can hope that if they have no reason to suspect they're being watched, they'll simply get off the boat sooner or later. That's what we have to wait for. After they get off we'll get them. I only hope the boys don't try anything else. That signal was smart, but it was dangerous too."

"These men don't seem too smart," said Walt.

"Men like that are never smart," said the captain, "but that doesn't make them any the less dangerous. They won't get away, they wouldn't have anyhow, but right now that's not the point. The point is getting them off that boat with no harm done."

Mrs. Slocum started to cry quietly.

"I think you'd better go," said the captain, "and believe me we know what we're doing, so don't worry." He grinned. "I know you will, of course, but everything'll come out all right."

They all left Mr. Lawson's office except Walt and Mr. Lawson and Captain Logan.

"What do you really think, Captain?" asked Walt.

"I told you what I thought," said the captain, "that's just about it."

"What do you think their chances are?"

"Good. As long as they don't get those mad dogs suspicious."

"They'll try something," said Walt; "I know them."

"Well you'd better hope they don't." The captain sighed suddenly. "I have two boys of my own. Maybe I shouldn't have been so honest about it

to the folks, but that's the way I would've wanted
it."

"I'm glad you did, Captain. May I stay with
you?"

"Who are you?"

"Walt Hadley, Win's my brother."

The captain studied him. "All right. It may be
a good idea. Then you can keep your family in-
formed."

"Good."

"Now," said the captain as he turned to Mr.
Lawson, "I'm going to need your help."

"Given," said Mr. Lawson simply.

"We can't use a patrol boat—that's obvious.
How many different kinds of boats do you have
here?"

Mr. Lawson laughed. "I see you ain't no boatman, Captain. We got hundreds of kinds; what do
you want?"

"Just different types, so we can pass them without being conspicuous."

"That'll be easy," said Mr. Lawson. "The
trouble is other boats. They'll see that there flag
upside down and they might try to help."

"Then we'll patrol in your boats and make sure
they don't. I'll get my troopers to wear regular
boating clothes. Mr. Hadley, can you run a powerboat?"

"Yes."

"Good. I'll change my clothes and you'll be my skipper. Do you have one with ship-to-shore radio?" he asked Mr. Lawson.

"Plenty. I'll give you a boat that'll do almost forty knots. Don't you worry about the boat."

The phone in the office rang and Mr. Lawson answered it. "For you." He handed the phone to the captain.

"Yes?" He listened for a while. "All right. Stay out of sight. I don't want them to see any uniforms." He hung up.

"They're heading in here. Probably to gas up. Now I want everything to be absolutely normal. Who usually pumps the gas?"

"All of us," said Mr. Lawson, "or one of my kids."

"I'll do it," said Walt.

Captain Logan thought that over. "No," he said, "the boys are liable to get excited when they see you and do something silly."

"No, they won't," said Walt; "these are smart kids. Not only that—I would recognize anything funny they told me. You wouldn't, you don't know them, but with me they could say all sorts of things that could be a message."

"It's an idea," said the captain.

"They're about a half mile off," said Mr. Lawson, peering out the window; "they'll be here in about ten minutes."

"Obviously the two men don't know the boys live in Dixboro," said the captain, "or they wouldn't put in here."

"Might have to," said Mr. Lawson, "might be short on fuel."

"How about it, Captain?" said Walt, speaking decisively. "It'll be the best thing, I'm sure of it."

"I admit you're likely to get information from them," said the captain. "What I want to know is could you get an idea across to them?"

"I could try," said Walt. "I'll be very careful not to say anything that would sound suspicious to those two men."

"Well . . ." the captain hesitated.

"Here they come," said Mr. Lawson.

"All right," said the captain. "Go ahead. And good luck."

"You wouldn't kid me, would you, sonny?" asked Buford.

"Well, you can check for yourself," said Scoop. "We'll go dry in about fifteen minutes more and there won't be any place to refuel."

"Can you make it to some gas station?"

"I can make it to Lawson's marina," said Scoop. "That's a mooring place for boats, in case you don't know," he added.

"All right, quiz kid," said Buford, then raised his voice. "Now listen, you fellers. We're going to get some gas. If anything happens, anything at all, ole Henry Smith going to fix up young Matt down here real good. Any questions?"

Nobody said anything.

"Fine," said Buford, "real fine. Just don't forget it."

There were no other boats at the dock and Scoop docked neatly and Win jumped off and tied up.

"Get back on," said Buford from the hatch. Win got back on.

A man was coming down the dock and Buford ducked into the cabin and closed the hatch, leaving a small aperture so he could peer out.

Both Win and Scoop recognized Walt Hadley immediately. He was wearing old clothes and a beat-up baseball cap.

"Gas, fellows?" he said cheerily.

Please, said Win to himself, *please, Walt, don't ask anything, don't do anything, please, Walt!*

Walt didn't. He stood there looking at them, grinning foolishly. "Well?"

"Uh, yeah," said Scoop. "Fill up the port and starboard tanks."

"Sure thing," said Walt and passed the hose over to Win.

"Great day for boating," said Walt. "Ain't much wind for that thing though."

"No," said Win, beginning to understand what was going on.

"Going far?"

"Oh, up the river a ways," said Win as casually as he could.

"Doing a little gunkholing," said Scoop, and Win saw he understood too that Walt was playing some kind of role.

"That's a pretty rugged little sloop you got there," said Walt, looking professionally at the hull. "Wouldn't be dangerous no matter where you went, with that hull."

"No, it's real rugged," said Win, watching him closely.

"Yeah," said Walt with the air of the professional, "rugged; no danger with that there hull."

"It's a good one," said Scoop.

"Course a fellow's got to watch a boat like yours real close," said Walt, "see nothing happens to it. You know—rocks, shoals, things like that."

"That's right," said Win.

"Yeah," said Walt blandly. "Got to watch it real close so nothing happens to lose it or nothing. Boats can be dangerous if you don't know what you're doing. I seen plenty of guys with nice new boats did foolish things with 'em and something happened. Handled the whole thing wrong, didn't know no better, and bang, the whole rig on the rocks or something."

"Oh, we're real careful," said Win, "we wouldn't want to lose this boat."

"Yeah, that's the right idea all right, all right," said Walt. "Not only the boat, I seen plenty of people get hurt 'cause they didn't handle a boat right. The other day this fellow was going up-river just like you and a big storm come up and he thought he'd go chargin' right on through it, sails up and everything, tried a lot of fool tricks with his nice new boat, and you know what happened?"

"What?" asked Scoop and his show of interest was quite real.

"He went right on the Pennetonck Rocks and got hurt real bad. Didn't think they'd save him for a while."

"Gee," said Win, "that's rough."

"Well, I don't like to be hard about it," said Walt, "but that's what a fellow gets for playing tricks when he should know better. He should've had somebody that knew what he was doing at least watching him."

"Well," said Win, "we wouldn't do anything foolish like that. We've all had quite a lot of experience."

"Well, that's all right then," said Walt, "as long as you know what's going on." He looked casually at Win.

"Oh, we know what's going on, all right," said Win. "We know pretty well what we're doing." He handed the hose back to Walt. "That's it, I guess, the tanks are full."

Scoop fished in his pockets and paid Walt for the gas.

"Thanks," said Walt, "take it easy now."

"Don't worry," said Win, "we will."

Scoop started the engine and Walt threw the lines off.

"So long," said Walt with a lazy wave of his hand.

"See you later," said Win.

When they were back out in the middle of the river Buford stuck his head out of the hatch. "That was real good, boys," he said; "I'm real proud of you."

"Thanks," said Win shortly.

Buford chuckled. "Don't get sore, sonny, they ain't nothing you can do about nothing." He looked at Scoop. "You say we should tie up at dark?"

"It's too dangerous to go on at night," said Scoop. "You heard what he said about the rocks and shoals. You can't see them at night." He didn't mention that there was a signal light at all the dangerous spots.

"You know where to stop?"

"I thought of another marina further . . ."

"Oh no, sonny, don't start getting smart on me now. We anchor just like you fellows was doing last night."

"Okay," said Scoop.

"That's right, okay," said Buford. "You fellers had it easy so far, don't start getting ideas."

"Oh, we won't," said Win.

"Good feller," said Buford, grinning at him wickedly.

"Buford?" It was Henry's voice from the cabin.

"Shut up."

"But Buford!"

"All right, what is it?"

"I'm getting sick down here. These here fumes from the engine like to smother me."

"Well, stay there anyhow," said Buford, unmoved.

There was a pause. "Buford?"

Buford didn't answer.

"Buford?"

"What!"

This time Henry's voice was quite different. It was still thin, but it wasn't whiny any more. It was cold and deadly and very quiet. "Buford, I said I wanted to come up for some air, and Buford, I am coming up."

Win, watching with interest, was struck by the threat in Henry's voice. He saw with surprise a sudden spasm of fear cross over Buford's face.

"Okay, Henry," said Buford, placatingly, "if it's that bad come on up."

He got out of the way and Henry came up on deck and sat down in the cockpit taking deep breaths of air.

Win and Scoop looked at each other. So,

thought Win, Buford is scared of Henry. It was a surprise to Win, but it sobered him too. Because, he thought, if Buford is scared of Henry, then he must be really dangerous. That's what Walt was trying to say, that's why he said no tricks.

Win had been thinking over what Walt had said. The message had been quite clear: they were being watched. But Win had been watching the shore and the passing boats and he had seen no sign of a patrol boat. Just regular power cruisers and an occasional sailboat. After seeing Buford's reaction to Henry he could now fully understand Walt's warning. Sit tight, wait, don't do anything!

CHAPTER EIGHTEEN

A Trap Is Sprung

"WHY DON'T YOU just go after them, Captain?" asked a reporter. "They're sitting ducks."

"So are those boys," said Captain Logan. "We'll wait."

They were using a marina upriver from Dixboro as headquarters.

Every three or four hours, Walt and the captain would go upriver in the powerful cruiser and pass the *Four Winds* at a good distance while the captain would study the boat with high-powered glasses.

Along shore, following the boat's slow progress up the river, there was quite a to-do. Troopers were everywhere, ready to spring into action at any moment in any place should the two men decide to leave the boat. Many people were watching the boat through binoculars, opera glasses, telescopes—anything they could find.

Captain Logan had forbidden any broadcasts

over the local radio about his operation and of course the stations had co-operated, in fact were having an interesting time busily manufacturing newscasts designed to lull the two bandits into a false sense of security.

All other boats in the area had been warned by the state troopers to stay away from the little sloop and above all to ignore the distress signal flying from the mainmast.

In the upriver marina, the temporary headquarters, Captain Logan, a lieutenant named Forsythe, Walt and Mr. Lawson were sitting around a table. The reporters had been dismissed and Captain Logan was summing up the situation, being constantly interrupted by the telephone at his elbow as troopers from boats and along the river bank kept him up to date on the progress of the sloop.

"How much farther can he go, Mr. Lawson?" asked the captain.

"Not much farther," said Lawson. "Tonight is the last one I would say."

"But the river goes another twenty or thirty miles," said the captain. "Why won't they continue tomorrow?"

" 'Cause the river ain't navigable beyond Littler's Point. Too shallow for the *Four Winds*. The river's only about a foot or two deep up there. The boat draws over three. No, they ought to reach Littler's Point by dark, but that'll be it. They ain't goin' no farther even if they want to."

"Okay," said the captain, "we'll think of concentrating our troopers up there. Lieutenant, why don't you take charge of that right now, so we'll be good and ready. The whole works—walkie-talkies, big spotlights—you know. And keep in touch."

"Yes, sir," said the lieutenant, and went out.

"What's the plan, Captain?" asked Walt.

"Well it's simple enough," said the captain, "mostly because it depends on what those two birds do. If they get off alone and try it through the woods it'll be a snap. But if they take one of those boys as a hostage it won't be so easy."

"Then what?" asked Walt worriedly.

"Well, we got to get those birds, Mr. Hadley. We'll do it real carefully but we've got to do it. I only hope they've been listening to some of the phony broadcasts those crazy announcers are cooking up."

"I'm sure they are," said Mr. Lawson. "They sure ought to be interested in 'em. Besides, young Slocum's too good a sailor not to want to hear the weather report."

"If they let him," said Walt morosely.

"Yeah," said Mr. Lawson, "if they let him."

"Well," said the captain, "we might as well take another spin in that bomb of Mr. Lawson's. See

if everything's the same. I'd sure like to know for
sure what's going on on that boat."

On the boat they were doing just what Captain
Logan wanted them to do. They were listening
to the radio newscast.

"And so, another day is passing with no sign of
the fugitives," said the deep-voiced newscaster.
"The bloodhounds went as far as the Wyandot
River and then seemed to lose the scent. It was an
isolated spot, so it is thought that the men may
have tried to swim a ways to throw the dogs off.
But no further trace of the men has been found
and there are some unofficial opinions that the
men might even have drowned in the treacherous
currents of the river. However the hunt goes on.
Captain Logan, of the State Police Barracks in
Crawford is in charge of the search. He said early
this afternoon to this reporter that he felt the men
had somehow doubled back and were heading east
toward Boston. A large concentration of local police and state troopers have set up countless roadblocks on all roads leading to Boston. Captain
Logan confidently expects an arrest within twenty-
four hours. And now a word from your friendly
butcher . . ." Buford snapped the set off.

"Hey, hey," he said and slapped Henry on his
skinny back. "How 'bout that, Henry? I believe
we went and flummoxed 'em! They looking on
land and we on the river." He came farther up

the hatchway. "We're real grateful to you fellers. Ain't we, Henry?"

"Yeah, Buford," whined Henry. He was feeling much better although he was still sitting in the cockpit.

"Yessir, fellers, if we wasn't such poor fellers we might give you a share of the loot. But we been without for a long spell so we'll just keep it." He motioned to Scoop. "You still say tonight's the last night?"

"Well, it's the last night for the boat, that's for sure," said Scoop. "We can't go past Littler's Point in this boat. It's too shallow."

"You wouldn't be getting tired of us, would you, sonny? Is that why you say we can't go no farther?" He laughed. "Henry and me has really enjoyed our stay. It ain't been bad at all. Good food, nice dry boat, blankets, everything. In fact I might buy me a boat when I get where I'm going."

"Where's that?" asked Win.

Buford chuckled. "Oh I couldn't say sonny, at least not for publication as you might say."

A powerboat passed about three hundred yards away, going a good twenty knots. Win looked at it and suddenly realized that this same powerboat had passed several times. He studied it more closely and then he recognized it. It was Mr. Lawson's pride, a heavy forty-five-foot cruiser. He glanced at Scoop who caught it and nodded. Scoop too had recognized the boat, and if Win knew Scoop, he had probably recognized it earlier but had had no chance to tell the others.

It had been a very long, confining day they had spent. One of the men held the gun while the other got some sleep. The efficient way they went about it showed they had done it before sometime, somewhere. At any rate, their quick adaptability to the boat and its very limited confines showed that they were men who had done a lot of living on the move. They slept easily and lightly and any time they felt like it. And when they were on guard they were wide-awake and constantly watchful.

Win realized that tonight was the crucial time. He had tried to think of some way to catch the men off guard, but they were simply too alert and offered no opportunities for any kind of an attack. Win hoped that they would just leave the boat that night and nothing would be lost but some time and gas and food. He knew for sure that when they did debark finally, there would be some very serious people who would be very happy to greet them. Win would have tried anything within reason, but as he knew now, these were by no means reasonable men. He, for one, would be quite content to get them off the boat as soon as possible and he was sure the others felt the same way. It had been quite an adventure but it had lasted long enough and he didn't like these men at all. They were vicious and mean, and for the first time in his life, Win knew what it felt like to hate somebody. Especially Buford with his constant talk and nasty sarcasm and his threats. Well, thought Win, one way or the other, it'll be all over tonight.

The phone rang at Captain Logan's elbow. "Yes?" He listened attentively. "All right, I'll be right out." He turned to Walt. "They're about twenty minutes from Littler's Point." He smiled at Walt. "I imagine you would like to come?"

"I sure would."

"I thought so. Come on." As they climbed into the trim squad car, Captain Logan said, "You've been a great help, Mr. Hadley. You handled that scene at the dock very well."

"Thanks," said Walt. "I was more than happy to help."

"Well, I must say, Mr. Hadley, if you ever decide to give up your occupation we could use you at the barracks. I mean that, Mr. Hadley."

"Walt," said Walt.

"What?"

"The name is Walt. And thank you for the compliment."

"You're welcome, Walt."

They drove at top speed to Littler's Point.

It was quite a scene. Everything had been

planned in advance, and although there had been feverish activity earlier, everything was now quiet. There were local police and troopers everywhere, heavily armed, but it was hard to see them. They were dispersed over a large area and they were lying in the brush, well concealed. There was no talking. They just waited.

Walt had not seen the captain really in action before, and it was an impressive sight. He took complete charge at once, and with the lieutenant and two local police chiefs he went quietly over the plans, giving directions with a minimum of words and a maximum of effect. He checked by walkie-talkie with the various flanking points, then satisfied that everyone knew what he must do, he picked up a big spotlight, and with the walkie-talkie slung around his neck, walked to the river's edge. Here, he and Walt crouched behind a big boulder. The boat was not yet in sight, it had to come around a wide bend in the river.

It was late and the light was gradually failing. It would be night within the hour.

"How far out will they have to anchor, Walt?" asked the captain.

"At least fifty yards," said Walt, "maybe more."

"They'll probably use the dinghy to row in then."

"Yes," said Walt, then paused. "I hope everything works out all right."

"So do I, Walt," said the captain, "so do I."

They waited in silence for another few minutes.
"There they are," said Walt, "here they come."

The little boat came around the bend and pro-
ceeded steadily up the river. From the many men
on the bank there was not a sound. Hundreds of
alert eyes watched the little sloop as it finally
swung in toward the bank. As Walt had predicted,
they came in until they were about fifty yards from
the bank, then Win chucked the anchor over the
side. Scoop reversed the engine slowly until he
was sure the anchor was properly set, then he shut
off the engine.

The sudden quiet was startling. It was a deserted stretch, with the slopes down to the bank
heavily wooded.

The watchers could hear the sound of voices
from the boat, but they couldn't make out the
words. Walt watched closely. He saw Win and
Scoop, and there was a little man in the cockpit
who had to be Henry Smith. For a few moments
Walt could not see the other man, then he saw
him standing on the hatch ladder with just part
of his head visible. He couldn't see Matt at all, so
he must be in the cabin. The boys looked all right;
so far evidently the two men had done nothing to
harm them. *I hope everything goes smoothly,* said
Walt to himself, *I hope those boys don't get hurt.*

"We'll wait till it's dark," said Buford, "so
Matt, sonny, you might as well make us up one

of them famous meals of yours. We'll have a fare-well party."

"There isn't much left," said Matt.

"Well, whatever there is, sonny, make sure Henry and me gets it. Don't know when we'll be eating again."

"I don't like it," said Henry suddenly, and he moved uneasily in the cockpit.

Buford studied the shore for a few moments, then looked at Henry. "What's the matter, Henry? I don't see nothing."

"Me neither," said Henry, "but I don't like it."

They all looked at the shore. Nothing moved but a few birds, high in the trees, and there was no noise except for the faraway bark of a dog.

Buford was getting a little worried. It was obvious that he respected Henry's instincts. "Just what is it, Henry?"

"They ain't nothing," said Henry, "that's one of the reasons I don't like it. Don't like the feel of it neither. Don't like it at all."

Win watched Henry. He was like an animal, he was sniffing the light evening breeze, his nostrils flaring. His eyes roamed the bank carefully, back and forth. Win knew there must be men in there. Henry couldn't know, but his instincts were tugging at him. Win looked at the shore. He couldn't see a thing that looked at all out of order. But Henry was nervous and he kept searching the shore with his bright little eyes.

"Aw," said Buford and tried to dispel his own uneasiness with a short laugh. "Aw, they ain't nothing there, Henry. You just nervous about getting off."

"I ain't saying there's anybody in there," said Henry, "I'm just saying I don't like it. Something wrong somewhere."

"Well, let's eat," said Buford, "maybe you'll feel better."

"You say," said Henry, and Win noticed the whine in his voice had disappeared again. "You say," repeated Henry, "but I got a feel."

There was just enough food for the two men and while they were eating Buford talked.

"You see, fellers, I got to pay attention to Henry when he says things like that. He ain't right all the time, but he sure is right a lot of times." His voice held a strange sort of respect and admiration as he discussed Henry's strange talents. "He can sniff out a cop, or a thief, don't matter which, a mile away. We was in a hotel down South once, we was just laying on the bed trying to figure whether to go or to stay, and Henry all at once gets up and says, 'Let's go,' and I asks why, and he says because there's some cops coming, so we go and, by golly, we was just driving away and a police car drives up in front of the hotel." He looked around at the boys so they could share his enthusiasm, then at little Henry. "Now ain't that something? He's got himself a nose all right, all right. Got to pay attention when Henry says something like that. Don't say nothing else, Henry don't—real stupid—but he's got himself a nose."

Henry just sat there not saying anything. He didn't seem to mind at all when Buford called him stupid.

"Well, what are you going to do, then?" asked Win.

"Oh we'll get off at dark," said Buford. "They ain't nothing else to do. But we may have to change our plans a little."

"What do you mean?" asked Matt.

"I figure one of you has to come along," said Buford casually. "I figure we might need some protection if Henry's nose is right."

"Wait a minute," said Win, "you can't do that. He might get hurt."

"That's right, sonny, he might. It's a rough life, that's for sure."

"Look," said Win, "we haven't harmed you. We've done a lot for you. You've taken our boat, you've eaten all our food. Why don't you just leave us alone now?"

"Don't get riled up, sonny," said Buford. "Don't get me riled neither."

"One of us would just slow you down," said Win, "you'd be much better off without another guy."

Buford stopped chewing and looked thoughtfully at Win. "Sonny," he said, "do I tell you how to run a boat? No, I don't. So don't tell me how to do something I know a lot more'n you do about. Another thing. You been a good boy so far, now you're starting to get just a little bit under my skin."

"Look," said Win, trying desperately to get him to change his mind. That was as far as he got. Buford, with disconcerting swiftness, leaned over and slapped Win hard across the face with his open palm. It was a blow with real force, and Win was knocked back off the bunk and against the bulkhead. Win was suddenly flooded with rage. He pushed hard against the bulkhead trying to get to his feet.

"Don't," said Henry quietly, bringing up the gun.

"Win!" yelled Matt and grabbed his arm. "Take it easy, Win."

"That's right, sonny," said Buford, "you tell him. I guess maybe what I say goes. I don't want to remind you no more." He calmly continued eating.

For the first time since they had been commandeered by the two men, Win was really angry and not in the least afraid. The anger had burned away his fear, but even so he was grateful to Matt for stopping him. He had seen Henry's eyes, and he was virtually certain the little man would have shot him. He had no previous experience to call on in a situation like this, but there was no mistaking the look on Henry's face. It was mean.

"We'll take the little one," said Buford, indicating Scoop. "He ain't likely to be as much trouble as you two big fellers."

Nobody said anything, and after the two men had finished eating it was dark and Buford motioned them all on deck.

"We going to leave in about five minutes," he said to Scoop, "so pull that little boat up here and you can row us in." He pointed to the others. "You two stay right here, and I don't want to hear no noise or your buddy's gonna get hurt. Okay?"

"Okay," said Matt after a moment.

"Fine," said Buford.

"It ain't," said Henry, speaking in his sudden way.

"What ain't?"

"It ain't fine. I tell you, Buford, I *feel* something."

"You want to stay here?" asked Buford.

"No," said Henry, "no sense to that, I know, but still I'm mighty uneasy in my stomach."

"We'll have the kid," said Buford, "that ought to help."

"Yeah," said Henry, but he was very nervous; "maybe."

"All right," said Buford, "no sense waiting. Let's get going."

They pulled the dinghy in by the painter, and Scoop got in the boat. His face was drawn and white but he didn't argue. Buford got in next, stumbling clumsily and hanging onto the rigging of the sloop. Finally he was set in the stern. "Okay, Henry," he said, "hand me the gun, and get in."

Henry was standing at the edge of the gunwale and before he handed the gun to Buford he looked at the other two to make sure they were far enough away not to take advantage of the moment. Matt was in the hatchway, and Win was on the other side of the cabin, about eight feet away. Henry was about to hand the gun to Buford when they all heard it. It was a loud clack, the unmistakable sound of metal on metal and it carried clearly over the water.

Henry jerked erect and faced the shore, the gun coming up.

As he did so a powerful spotlight came on and caught them in the middle of its glare. "Hold it!" said a voice over a loud-speaker, shattering the quiet. Henry snarled something and raised the gun and aimed.

Without thinking, acting purely on reflex, Win came in a rush over the cabin top and hit Henry hard in a driving tackle.

They went bowling over the side, the gun flying from Henry's hand and dropping with a plop into the water.

Henry fought like a wild animal, biting and kicking and scratching. But Win was bigger and much stronger, and he was full of fight. All his anger and resentment, pent up over the last few hours, was released in a flurry of action.

More searchlights flashed on, and men rushed from the shore into the water. Around the bend in the river came several powerful boats, their lights on, fixing the little sloop in a bath of light, rushing at full speed toward the scene.

Scoop did a very simple thing. He merely dived into the water and, reaching up, he grabbed the gunwale of the little dinghy and capsized it and Buford was in the water too.

The men reached them in a matter of seconds and it was all over. Henry was dragged from the river shaking and spitting like a half-drowned rat. He was wild with rage and still fought, but he was soon subdued and handcuffed.

Buford was in not much better shape because when he had come to the surface after Scoop capsized the dinghy, he was all but obliterated by Matt who, in one flying leap, had landed right on top of him.

They all gathered on shore in the glare of the powerful lights.

Win rushed up to Walt and shook his hand. "Nice going, Walt!" he said, still full of the excitement. "We got them, we sure got them!"

"We sure did," said Walt. "Talk about excitement!"

Captain Logan came up to Win and held out his hand.

"We saw what you did, son, and there's no question that slamming Smith into the water like that saved somebody from getting hurt."

"I didn't even think," said Win, "I just did it."

"Well, there's a time for thinking and a time for acting," said the captain, "and you did both at the right times."

Scoop came rushing over. "What a scoop!" he shouted. "I finally get to live up to my name! A first-hand account! Maybe I'll get the Pulitzer Prize for Journalism!" He rushed off as quickly as he had come.

"You boys all did well," said the captain. "You kept your heads all the way after your little chat with Walt here. I congratulate you sincerely."

"Thanks," said Matt and Win.

"Now," said the captain, "you'd better get in touch with your folks. They're all pretty worried."

As they were leaving to make the telephone call, they passed Henry and Buford, handcuffed and standing between two tall state troopers.

"Nice going, kids," said Buford, and he didn't sound angry at all. "You did us in, all right, but I got to hand it to you, you done real good."

Henry Smith didn't say anything. He just stood there, wet and bedraggled, his bright eyes fixed on the boys in a steady unblinking stare.

The three friends looked thoughtfully at each other, then hurried off to call their families.

CHAPTER NINETEEN

The Semi-Finals

"Well, you sure have had an exciting summer," said Ed Partridge.

"And how," said Win. "I'm not sure I could go through another one like it."

They were sitting on the bench next to the center court at the Dixboro public courts.

"Well, Win," said Ed, "the State Finals are starting Monday. Do you think you're ready?"

"Yes," said Win, "I do."

"I do too, Win. We've done a lot of work this summer and we've come a long way. You're a lot better player now than you were three months ago. It may sound conceited, but I'm glad to have had a hand in it."

"A hand? You did it all, Ed."

"Not by a long shot, I didn't," said Ed. "As long as it's mutual admiration time, I might as well tell

you, without your native talent and your willingness to learn, it might have been a wasted summer."

"But it hasn't," said Win.

"No, it hasn't. There's something else I'd like to say. I don't like to intrude on your private affairs, but if you don't mind I think I'll mention it."

"I don't mind; go ahead."

"It's about Dan Slade. I don't know but what you two think this tournament is just an event for you two. Well it isn't. There are going to be a lot of very fine juniors from all over the state. You probably won't even play each other. The only way you will is if you both get into the finals. That's a long, tough road and both of you could be beaten before you get there. I just want you to forget Dan Slade and play each match as it comes along. If you get to the finals and he does too, all right. But remember the others that are trying to win too. One match at a time, remember."

"I will," promised Win. "I know it's going to be tough."

"It is, you can be sure of it. But I tell you truthfully you have an excellent chance. You're a fine player, the best I ever coached. As a matter of fact, I wouldn't be surprised that if you played Walter Williams now you might beat him. Next year you will almost certainly."

"You really think I have a good chance?"

"No question about it. If your desire is strong enough."

"I want to win it," said Win, "if that's what you mean."

"That's what I mean. You've got to want to win it badly. That sharpens your concentration and that's what you need. That's what you have, too; and believe it or not, I'm not too worried."

"Well I am," said Win.

"That's fine," said Ed, "you should be concerned. Confidence is fine, but overconfidence is the short way out of a tournament." He leaned back and looked out over the courts. "It's a great game, tennis, Win. I've been involved in it for years, and I don't regret it. I've never been much more than a good weekend player but even that's been enough for me. But you—you could go all the way. That would be thrilling." He was quiet for a while.

"I've seen them all. Forest Hills, Wimbledon, Paris and Rome. Not quite all. I've never been to Australia. I'd like to go some day." His voice quickened with enthusiasm. "Can you imagine a tennis stadium that holds over thirty thousand fans? That's what they have down there. They have the players too. Yes, it's a great game. Tilden and Johnson, Vinnie Richards, Ellsworth Vines, Fred Perry, Jean Borotra, Don Budge and Jack Kramer —I've seen them many times. And the modern ones today. Great, just great. They're champions, all of them, artists really, because it is an intensely individual performance. They're all alone out there with no one to help them, it's all up to them."

"I wish I could have seen some of them in their prime," said Win.

"It was something," said Ed, "but there are great ones today too. Maybe *you* some day."

"Do you think so, Ed, do you really think so? Oh, I know I play the game pretty well, but pretty well doesn't count at Forest Hills or Wimbledon."

"You're right, it doesn't." Ed considered for a moment. "I can't say for sure, Win, that you'll ever take that big cup out of the stadium at Forest Hills. But I can say, to the best of my knowledge and with some confidence in my judgment, that you have a chance to do it. Someday we'll see, that's all."

"Gosh," said Win, entranced by the thought, "wouldn't that be something!"

"It certainly would," said Ed, "it certainly would."

They were quiet for a while.

"All right," said Ed, "enough of this daydreaming. When you go up there for the tournament I want you to start thinking right away of what you're going to do in every situation. Saturate yourself with tennis, think tennis all the time, do what you've been taught, use your head, and for heaven's sake don't worry about Dan Slade until you have to. Remember he's worrying about you too."

"I'm not worried about Dan Slade," said Win.

"Good. But if you do play him, then you can do a little worrying. That boy is a mighty fine tennis player and unless I miss my guess you're going to be seeing a lot of him in the next few years. You'll both probably be in a lot of tournaments together."

"I'll do my best," said Win, and he meant it.

"I have every confidence that you will." Ed stood up. "I won't see you for a while. I'll try to get down for the finals, so try to be in them."

"Ed," said Win, "thanks. Thanks for everything." He felt a little sad, and he wasn't sure why. He would certainly see Ed Partridge again.

"Win, it's been a real pleasure. I mean it."

They shook hands and Win watched the gray-haired man with his brown face and erect figure walk off toward the clubhouse.

I was lucky, he said to himself, very lucky. There aren't many Ed Partridges around, and I was mighty fortunate that there was one around when I needed him.

On the way home, Win made a promise to himself. Whether or not he won the State Juniors, he was going to do everything Ed had taught him. He was going to remember everything, he was going to use his head as well as his muscles.

He wasn't going to let Ed Partridge down.

The Massachusetts State Junior Tournament was held at Holden College in Holden. They were using the Holden College courts which were set near the football stadium. It was a beautiful setting, the carefully tended lawns and athletic fields shining green and the mountains clear in the background.

Ed Partridge had been right about one thing. It was a big tournament and it wasn't going to be easy to win it.

Win saw Ralph Bates and Fred Atchison from Crawford High, Willy Smith from Edgartown and many other fine players who had been in the tournament the year before. And Dan Slade.

Win and Dan were in opposite halves of the draw, so unless they both made the finals, they would not play each other. The winner of each bracket played in the finals.

The first two or three rounds were not too difficult and Win won his matches handily. It was really little more than a warm-up session in each case.

But at the beginning of the fourth round, things got considerably more difficult. Win still advanced steadily in his bracket, but now he was forced to play his best tennis.

He had a very tough match with Fred Atchison from Crawford and although he won it in straight sets, it was a very close match.

Win was standing at the big board studying the results of the other matches after his match with Fred when Dan Slade came up.

They nodded to each other.

"I see you're still in it," said Dan, pointing to the board.

"You too," said Win. "Congratulations."

"Not yet," said Dan; "after the finals."

"I'd better wait then," said Win.

"Where's your gang?"

"My gang?"

"You know that gang of big heroes that goes around capturing bank holdup men."

"Oh," said Win, determined not to lose his temper. "Matt and Scoop. They'll be up over the weekend for the finals."

"Why?" asked Dan.

"Why?"

"Yes, why. You don't expect to be in it, do you?"

"I don't know," said Win calmly; "we'll see."

"I'll tell you something, Hadley, I hope you are."

"Thank you," said Win politely.

"You know what I mean," said Dan. "I want

you in the finals. I want to beat you. You were lucky last time."

"I know it," said Win. "Well, we'll see. If we get to the finals, that is."

"Well I'm going to get there," said Dan, "that's for sure."

Win turned away. "Well, good luck," he said.

"I don't need luck," said Dan, "I don't need anything but what I've got."

Win walked away without answering. If confidence was a valuable asset, Dan Slade ought to be able to beat anybody.

On Saturday, the day of the semi-finals, Matt and Scoop came up and met Win about two hours before he was to play. They drove up in Scoop's old pink jalopy and Matt said he was a nervous wreck and very happy and surprised to have made it at all. The rest of Win's fans were driving up with Walt and Mrs. Hadley. There were no matches to watch until Win played, so they went to a diner near the courts.

"So it's Willy Smith from Edgartown," said Matt. "If you'll excuse my grammar, that ain't easy."

"It sure isn't," said Win. "I'll have to pay attention to my knitting."

"What'll you have?" said Scoop. "I'm still rich from my famous international scoop."

"Well, as long as you're buying," said Matt, "I think I'll have a light lunch. I'll start with four hamburgers, two milkshakes, and maybe a couple of pieces of pie."

"What if I weren't buying?"

"I'd have a glass of water," said Matt. "I never eat on my own money."

"You eating, Win?" asked Scoop.

"I shouldn't have lunch until after my match," said Win, sniffing the delicious odors from the grill, "but I think I'll have one hamburger and a glass of milk. That shouldn't hurt."

"Since when did food hurt a growing boy?" said Matt. "Now about my lunch . . ."

"Eat up, son," said Scoop airily. "I'm a big spender from Texas."

"I accept," said Matt. "For some reason it tastes better when somebody else is paying."

"You sure ought to know," said Scoop with mock disgust.

They were all hungry and when the food came they ate with gusto.

"You might say we are eating these hamburgers with relish," said Scoop.

"Stop, please," said Matt; "you'll ruin my appetite with those jokes."

"Your appetite? Never."

"You know," said Win, looking at Matt's thick milkshake, "I think I'd better have one of those.

If there's one thing I miss up here, it's my mother's cooking. I think I'm slowly but surely starving to death."

Before Win was finished, he had had two hamburgers and two milkshakes, and after watching Matt and Scoop gobbling apple pie à la mode, he had some of that too. When he got up, he felt a little stuffed.

"Maybe I ate too much," he said. "Tom Joyce always said to eat light before a lot of action."

Matt was alarmed. "Hey," he said, "I hope not. I want you to wallop Dan Slade. You can't do that if you get put out."

"Oh, I'm all right," said Win. "I just ate a little too much. It'll wear off."

They went out into the hot sun. After the air conditioning of the diner, the heat had a wilting quality.

"Wow!" said Matt, "I wonder what the temperature is."

"It must be around ninety," said Scoop; "in the shade, that is. It's a lot hotter in this sun." And he squinted up at the sky. It was cloudless and the midsummer sun hung like a heavy, fiery ball overhead. There was not a whisper of a breeze and the driving heat from the sun pressed like a blanket on the three boys as they walked over to the Holden College courts.

Win went to the locker room to change and

Matt and Scoop went to look for the Hadleys, the Hugheses and Ed Partridge.

Win was the only one in the room; Willy Smith evidently had already dressed. He changed slowly, still feeling a little logy from the heavy lunch. By the time he was dressed he felt better and he went out to the court.

It was hot on the court but it must have been very uncomfortable in the stands. There was no shade and there were many straw hats and a variety of headgear fashioned from newspapers to protect the people from the broiling sun.

Win saw his family and friends sitting together, and he waved to them. Willy Smith was standing by the umpire's chair waiting for him, idly spinning his racket. He held out his hand.

"Hi, Win."

"Hi, Willy."

"Want to rally right now?"

"Sure," said Win, "might as well get started."

Willy got the new balls, white and fluffy and clean, and they went out onto the court and began to hit.

"This is a semi-final match," intoned the umpire into his microphone, "between, on my left, Winfield Hadley of Dixboro, Dixboro Junior Champion and last year a quarter-finalist in the State; on my right, Willy Smith of Edgartown, Junior Champion of Martha's Vineyard and also a quarter-finalist last year in the State Tournament."

They finished the rally and spun for serve. Willy won.

"Mr. Smith has won the spin," said the umpire in his very impersonal voice, "and will serve first. This is a best-two-out-of-three match." He looked at Willy. "Ready?"

"Ready," said Willy.

"Ready?" to Win.

"Ready."

"Play!"

Willy served and the match was on.

They played evenly for four games and it was good tennis. Willy Smith was a tall, thin, blond boy with his hair cut very short. He had been well coached and he knew what he was doing. His major weakness, Win soon discovered, was in his speed. He did very well with every ball he could reach, he stroked it well and made the right tactical shot, but he was slow in getting there. He had long legs and big feet, and although he could react swiftly to any ball hit near him, if he had to run any distance he got a slow start and, once started, didn't go very fast. Win naturally decided to exploit this weakness. He went back to receive service. They stood at two–all.

He anticipated where the serve was going and instead of blocking it back he drove it hard, catch-

ing Willy still in back court; then he rushed the
net. Willy, caught unaware, hit up a high, short
lob. Win stepped into it, hitting hard, squinting
into the bright sky. The ball whistled down into
the corner—a clean placement, and the crowd
applauded.

Win walked slowly back to receive again. Something had happened to him. With no warning, his
stomach was knotted with sharp pains and he felt
dizzy. The heat was suddenly a factor, and he
started to perspire heavily. He knew why too.
Those two hamburgers with lettuce and tomato
and mayonnaise, and two heavy, thick milkshakes,
then the swift action and the stifling heat. He
shook his head and set himself to receive, trying
to ignore the dizziness and the pains in his stomach.

Willy aced him on the serve. Win stood as if
rooted to the spot. He simply could not make his
body move fast enough, so he didn't move at all.

Willy took the next three points and the game.
Win didn't get another point after the first one.

As they changed courts, Willy glanced at him,
then did a double take. "Hey," he said with concern, "what's the matter?"

Large drops of perspiration were rolling down
Win's face, which was pale under his tan. "Nothing," he said, "I'll be all right. It's the heat."

The umpire peered down at him thoughtfully.
"Are you all right, Mr. Hadley?"

"Yes," said Win doggedly, wiped his face with a towel and went out to serve. He had a real attack of cramps now, and it was difficult to stand upright, let alone play a tournament game of tennis. The set deteriorated into a shambles. Win was too weak and sick to do anything. He lost his serve at love and by now the crowd knew very well that something was wrong. Win, going back to receive, saw Ed Partridge leave the stands and come down to the officials' table just off the center court where they were playing.

Willy went back to serve and ran the game out at love. The set stood at two–five and Win's serve. They walked around to change courts.

It was now impossible to ignore Win's condition. He was rolling as he walked, and he bent over at the waist to ease the cramps. The umpire climbed down from his chair. "Mr. Hadley," he said, "you can't continue in your present condition."

"Yes, I can," said Win.

"I suggest you forfeit," said the umpire. "You're in no shape to continue."

"Who calls the forfeit?" asked Win, his breath coming in labored gasps.

"Well," the umpire hesitated, "I believe the player is the judge of his own physical condition."

"All right, sir," said Win, "I'll continue."

"Why don't you rest awhile," said Willy, looking at him worriedly. "Maybe you'll feel better."

"I'm afraid that's against the rules," said the umpire; "but of course there is a short rest between sets."

"Come on, Willy," said Win trying to grin, "thanks for the try, but let's go."

So out they went and of course Win lost the game and the set six–two. Immediately he went over and sat down on the refreshment table behind the umpire's chair. The umpire climbed down and went off the court. Willy sat next to Win.

"Gee, Win," he said, "this is terrible."

"My fault," said Win. "I know better than to eat a big meal before a match. Especially in this heat."

"Are you going to make it?"

"I'm going to try," said Win, but he knew that unless the cramps went away he didn't have a chance. But he was determined not to quit.

The umpire came back and with him was Ed Partridge.

"What's the matter, Win?" asked Ed, and concern was plain on his face.

"I've got cramps," said Win, "and this heat doesn't help."

"Cramps?" Ed studied him for a moment. "You don't have a cold or anything, a fever?"

"No," said Win, reluctant to tell Ed what a foolish thing he had done.

"You didn't, by any chance, eat a heavy lunch, did you?"

Win nodded his head slowly. "Yes."

Ed made an impatient movement with his hand, then sighed. "Well, there's no point in telling you what a mistake that was. I guess you know it by now. The point is, can you play?"

"Sure," said Win. He didn't look to Ed as if he could.

"I regret very much to say this," said the umpire, "but the time allotted by the rules between sets has elapsed. I'm afraid we must continue or Mr. Hadley must forfeit the match."

"Give him a few more minutes," said Willy; "it's happened to me before. Sometimes they don't last long."

"I can't do that," said the umpire firmly, "a rule is a rule."

"He's right," said Ed; "that's what I would do if I were umpiring."

Win stood up, straightening with difficulty. "All right," he said, "I'm ready."

Ed looked at him and his pride in Win was written on his face. "You sure, Win?"

"I'm sure."

They went back on the court and into the blazing sun. Willy was serving. He won his serve at love for the second time. But for some reason the game took a long time for one that ended at love.

As they changed courts, Win said, "Cut it out, Willy."

Willy tried to look surprised. "Cut it out? Cut what out?"

"You know what I mean," said Win and took the balls from the ball boy and went to serve.

The cramps were less severe now and Win knew that if he only had enough time, he might be all right. But there wasn't much time.

Win lost his serve to Willy and again the game took a long time. Win knew why and he felt a warm rush of gratitude toward the tall, blond boy from Edgartown. Willy was not letting up on his shots, he was still driving them hard and deep, but he was hitting them right at Win and he wasn't rushing the net, so the result was a series of long base-line duels, long rallies that sometimes took several minutes. Win didn't have to run, he could stand virtually in the same spot and simply hit the ball back. Willy didn't throw the games, he made certain he won them, but the long rallies were giving Win the time he needed so much.

This pattern continued for some time, and Win got stronger and stronger. The cramps were nearly gone now and he could move almost at top speed again. But by that time he was down love–five in what could easily be the last set. As they changed for the sixth game, Win could feel the strength and rhythm of his body come back almost as suddenly as it had left him. As he passed Willy, Willy winked at him.

"You're all the way back now, aren't you?"

"Yes," said Win, "thanks to you."

"To me? What do you mean? I'm ahead five–love. That doesn't look very much like I've given you anything."

"All right," said Win, "we won't argue. Full speed?"

"Full speed," said Willy.

It was full speed all right and Win came back the hard way. He won his serve and it was his first game in the last ten. From then on Willy Smith gave him nothing. He had set point seven times in the set and lost them all to an inspired, fighting Win Hadley.

It was great tennis to watch. A comeback of the sort Win was putting on is rare against a player as good as Willy Smith, but come back he did. His serve was flashing in, his drives and volleys had their old crisp power and control, his drop shots and lobs were working for him perfectly. It was a complete reversal of form. And Willy Smith fought him every foot of the way. Their concentration was intense and the tennis was first-rate.

The crowd was delighted and the applause after a good point was loud and enthusiastic.

Win won the second set seven–five.

The third set was more of the same, and although Willy played the best he could, which was very good indeed, he simply didn't have the equipment to cope with Win. His lack of speed was finally the deciding factor. But he gave ground very slowly, and finally it was all over at six–four. Win was in the finals of the State Juniors.

He walked to the net and held out his hand. "Willy, I don't know why you did what you did, but I didn't deserve it."

"Heck, Win," said Willy, taking his hand, "I didn't want to back into the finals. I just am not made that way."

"You sure aren't, Willy," said Win. "It has been a great honor to play you, and I mean it sincerely when I tell you I wish it could have been the other way."

"Me, too," said Willy, grinning, "but when I win, I want to win the right way. You deserve it, anyhow. You're just too good for me."

They shook hands with the umpire and thanked him, then walked off the court. The first one to greet them was Ed Partridge. He held out his hand to Willy.

"I saw what you did, Willy," he said, and his voice was full of emotion. "I have never in thirty years of tournament tennis seen a more sportsman-like gesture. It was an exceptional thing for anybody to do, and from now on, Willy, you're the best in my book."

"Gosh," said Willy, reddening in embarrassment, "I'm getting more compliments for losing than I ever did for winning."

"You deserve it, son," said Ed, "listen to that."

The crowd was on its feet, and they were cheering and applauding, and it was all for Willy Smith. Win put his racket under his arm and began to applaud with them.

Willy blinked up at the noisy, demonstrative stands. Then he waved at them, his eyes filling with tears. "Wow," he said, "and I lost. Maybe I'd better lose from now on." But he was visibly affected and hurried into the locker room to hide his emotion.

Later, sitting in the stands with his family and friends, watching Dan Slade play Fred Atchison in the other semi-final, all Win could talk about was what Willy had done—and everyone there agreed with him.

"It had nothing to do with tennis," said Walt. "You're the better player—not by much, but you are. He simply wanted to beat you at your best or not at all."

"That's right," said Win.

"A fine young man," said Mrs. Hadley.

The match between Dan Slade and Fred Atchison was an anticlimax. Dan was not by any means at the top of his game but Fred was having a bad day too. He knew he would have to play at his best to win and the result was that he tried too hard. The match was close for almost two sets, simply

because they were both playing badly. In fact Win
had never seen Dan play with such listlessness and
he said as much to Ed Partridge.

"It's common enough," said Ed. "He knows he's
better than this Atchison boy and he's already
thinking of the finals tomorrow against you. The
mental attitude is almost as important as the physical in any sport and Dan just isn't concentrating."

Fred Atchison won the sloppily played set at
seven–five and evened up the match.

"Hey," said Scoop, "maybe Dan'll lose!"

"I hope not," said Win.

"You hope not? Why?"

"Because," said Win, "I've been waiting all
summer for a crack at him and this'll be my last
chance."

For a while in the third set it looked as if Dan
might lose at that. Fred, seeing a real chance to
beat him the way he was playing, began to take
advantage of Dan's lapses, and built up a four–
two lead. Then all at once Dan seemed to realize
what was happening to him and began to concentrate. Fred didn't win another game. Dan began
to play the way he could when he was concentrating, and it was quite an exhibition. He was a different player. He ranged all over the court, his
shots singing over the net, and his serves blasting
in again and again. He almost literally swept Fred
off the court with his power and volleying. The
crowd looked in amazement at a completely re-

juvenated Dan Slade. The set ended at six–four and the match was Dan's. The players went to the net to shake hands.

"Boy," said Win, "those last four games were really something."

"He's a mighty good player, Win," said Ed thoughtfully. "You're going to have to really pour it on to beat him."

"Don't worry," said Matt blandly, "the honor of his friends is at stake. Win won't let the boys down."

"That has very little to do with it," said Ed, "with a player as strong as Dan. He wants to win just as badly, I'm sure of it."

"So am I," said Win, "I've been waiting and so has he."

On the way out, Win saw Willy Smith and went over to him.

"Thanks again for the break," he said.

"Forget it," said Willy, "smartest thing I ever did. I'm a hero. Good luck tomorrow."

"Thanks," said Win, "I'm going to need it."

"You sure are," said Willy and grinned. "If you beat Willy Smith you got to be good. But so is Dan Slade. Real good."

"That's what everyone is telling me," said Win, "and I know it from experience."

So that's the way it was. Win Hadley and Dan Slade in the finals on Sunday, just as most people had predicted.

CHAPTER TWENTY

The Finals

THE WEATHER Sunday was perfect, with little wind and a cloudless sky. The stands were filled with an interested and festive crowd. It had been an exceptionally good tournament, many people had stayed over for the finals, and they were in an expectant and anticipatory mood.

They were not disappointed.

The finals match between Win and Dan was one that would be discussed for years to come.

They spun rackets for serve and Dan won and elected to serve. They had a brief warm-up, then the umpire said, "Ready, Mr. Slade?"

"Ready," said Dan.

"Ready, Mr. Hadley?"

"Ready," said Win, and the match began.

From the beginning the pattern was set. Both players were at the top of their game. Their shots were booming off the rackets with a clean, crisp sound, and the services were tremendous and tricky.

They played evenly, brilliant shots were the rule rather than the exception, and the games mounted steadily until the first set stood at nine–all. So far there was little to choose between the two. Dan won his serve at nine–all and went ahead ten–nine. It was typical of the set. Neither had lost his serve; to do so was almost the same as losing the set. Unless of course, the one who lost his serve could break back in the next game. But the way the two were serving, it was very unlikely.

Then Win did lose his serve. Nothing went wrong, he didn't make any mistakes; it was simply a question of several impossible breaks happening all at once.

They stood at thirty–all, then back and forth to deuce again. At deuce, the first break occurred. Win had slammed in his first serve and Dan leaped at it, just trying to get his racket on it. The ball hit the wood of his racket and flubbed into the net. Win was sure the point was over, when the ball, spinning crazily, seemed to climb the net by itself and drop over on Win's side. It was useless to try for it and it made the score set point. Win watched the ball drop, shook his head and went back to serve.

Again he hit a hard driving serve, again Dan hit it badly. This time Win rushed to the net, in case the same thing happened. It did. The ball

ran along the top of the net for about two feet,
then dribbled off, straight down. Win tried to
just touch it over. It was a very difficult shot, the
ball had to be hit almost straight up because it
had landed at the very base of the net. Win flicked
his racket and the ball went up and over, but just
as the crowd began to shout in delight, the umpire said into his microphone, "Touch!" Win
had touched the net with his racket, just lightly,
but it was against the rules and the point was jus-
tifiably given to Dan.

"No!" shouted some people in the stands. They
were certain Win had made the shot cleanly. Win
immediately waved his racket at the crowd, then
hit the net with it to show that the call had been
correct.

"Game and first set to Mr. Slade, eleven games
to nine," said the umpire. "Change courts."

As they changed, Dan said, "I suppose you think
that was luck?"

"What would you call it?" asked Win.

Dan didn't say anything for a moment, then he
said briefly, "Luck."

It was bad luck but there was nothing to be
done about it. Win walked out to receive for what
could very well be the last set. As he walked he
gave himself a talking to.

*Come on now, Win Hadley, so you lost a set.
You're playing well, keep concentrating, keep try-*

ing, remember all you've learned this summer. Now's the time, there won't be another one in this tournament. This, he said to himself, *is very definitely it.*

He won the second set.

He won it the hard way, with hard, flat drives, clever lobs, little drop shots, and, most of all, by sheer drive. He won it by tremendous expenditure of energy, he ran all over the court, he tried for everything. Dan played with him all the way; he gave slowly, very slowly, but Win's play was inspired and finally Win broke Dan's serve in the fifteenth game and went on to win it nine–seven. It had been another sparkling, brilliant set and the crowd was more than delighted. They had come for good tennis, but not even in their most optimistic moments had they expected the caliber of tennis and of competition that they were witnessing.

As they were resting before the last set, Win looked up into the stands and saw Matt and Scoop sitting with Mrs. Hadley and Tom Joyce and Ed Partridge. Pat Hughes was there too. Matt and Scoop were standing, they were both red in the face from their cheering and from the excitement. They were waving at Win; he could hear Scoop clearly shouting, "Come on, Win, go, go, go!"

Win needed that short rest. The last set had taken a lot out of him. The sun was hot and the heat was bouncing off the light-brown clay. He sucked on an orange and began to concentrate on the coming set.

They took up right where they had left off. It seemed impossible that the two of them could continue such inspired playing, but they did, and they kept the crowd in a constant uproar with their great shots.

On and on it went, even all the way, with first Dan making a beautiful smash and then Win, or a delicate high lob, a great retrieve, another lob or a drive of tremendous power for a clean placement. The serves were booming in and they both held their service again and again. Win's breath was coming in great gasps and his legs felt fluttery when he stood still. He was afraid for a moment that he was going to run out of strength, then he looked across the net and saw that Dan Slade was gasping for breath too. He's in no better shape than I am, said Win to himself, and went back to the battle.

There was a certain grimness to the match now. Both players were in a world of private concentration and drive. Neither of them quit for any ball and their clothes were stained with the clay from the court where they had fallen or slid in some desperate attempt to get a ball. It couldn't go on forever, someone had to win; but for several hours that afternoon it seemed as if it might go on forever.

Finally, with the score knotted again at nine–all, the first break came.

Dan double faulted twice in a row on his service and was down love–thirty. Win gripped his racket so tight his knuckles whitened. He might never get this close again and he knew it.

On the next serve he threw caution to the winds and instead of just blocking Dan's big serve, he anticipated correctly where it was coming, his backhand, and he stepped into it with all his power and drove it straight down the alley line. Dan didn't have a chance for it. The ball hit right on the base line and white chalk flew into the summer air.

Love–forty. Game point.

Dan got the next two points, hitting a service ace, and an overhead smash. Thirty–forty. It was still game point.

The next point took almost five minutes but finally Win threw up a little short lob as Dan came rushing to the net—and that was the game.

The crowd went wild. All Win had to do was hold his serve and he had only lost it once all afternoon. Up in the stands Scoop and Matt were beside themselves.

Win stood at the service line, trying to keep his fine edge of concentration. The noise was so great that the umpire had to ask twice for silence. Slowly the excited crowd quieted.

"Play," said the umpire.

Win served. Dan certainly wasn't quitting. His back was to the wall and he was using every ounce of desire and ability he possessed to break Win's service and get back even. He almost did it too. Almost.

The game lasted for almost fifteen minutes. Back and forth hummed the ball, point after point for each player, deuce, advantage, deuce, advantage, deuce, advantage.

Three times Win had match point, and lost it when Dan fought his way back to deuce. At least five times Dan had game point, the point that would even the match again, and lost them all.

It was a soft hit on a tremendous first service that finally did it. Dan tried to lob but it was too short and Win, knowing for sure that this was it, stood under it waiting for it to drop, then hit it with all his strength, and the stinging overhead smash went in cleanly for the placement.

"Game, set and match," said the umpire, but nobody heard him. "Game, set and match, to Mr. Hadley. He wins nine–eleven, nine–seven, nine–seven." The umpire knew no one was listening but he didn't care. He was thrilled by it all too.

Win walked up to the net to meet Dan. He held out his hand and Dan shook it.

"Congratulations," said Dan with no emotion.

"Thank you," said Win, and hesitated. "Dan?"

"Yes?" Dan looked at him coolly.

"Dan, it's the greatest match I've ever played

in. You are without a doubt the best junior I've ever played against."

"Yes," said Dan, "I believe you're right."

Then the committee chairman came over and broke them up, congratulating both of them. The man's face was red and he was most pleased with the great finals match. "Best ever!" he kept saying over and over again. Then he led them in front of the stand where the presentations of the cups were to be made.

As he looked up into the stand, Win saw something he never would have believed. Ed Partridge, the calm, sedate man, was waving and shouting, his hair awry and his face flushed. He waved violently at Win and clasped his hands over his head. Win waved his racket at him and laughed at the spectacle. It touched him very much, that Ed had felt so strongly about him.

After the presentations and pictures, Dan and Win walked off the court, amid an enthusiastic round of applause, and into the locker room. The door closed behind them and they were alone.

Win slumped down on the bench in front of his locker. Now that the tremendous effort was over, he felt drained. Dan sat down too and stared at the floor. They just sat there for a while, too tired to move. Then Dan got up slowly and came over to Win. He looked down at him.

"That was really something," he said.

Win looked at him. "It sure was," he said.

"I have to admit it," said Dan, "you're a better player than I am. I never played better and I lost."

"I never played better either," said Win, "and I was lucky to win."

"You weren't lucky. Sure you played the best you ever did but so did I. And you won. So that's that." He sat down next to Win. "You know, Hadley, I envy you."

"Me?" Win was startled. "Why?"

"I'm not sure. But I do." He grinned shame-facedly at Win, then got up and started stripping for his shower.

Win looked after him in surprise. Why Dan Slade should envy him was something he didn't understand at all.

Dan didn't say any more about it, but as they prepared to leave the locker room he held out his hand.

"Congratulations, again," he said, "and I really mean it. That match was one of the most exciting things that ever happened to me."

"Me, too, Dan; it was really something."

"Well, so long."

"So long, Dan. See you at football practice. It starts in a week."

"That's right," said Dan, "and there's one thing about football."

"What do you mean?"

"We'll be on the same side, anyhow." He laughed and went out.

CHAPTER TWENTY-ONE

From Tennis to Croquet

"WELL, I must say," said Mrs. Hadley, "this has been quite a summer for you boys."

"It certainly has," said Tom Joyce, putting down a tall glass of iced tea. "The big struggle with Dan's boat, that incredible day with the two holdup men, Scoop's scoop that was printed all over the country, and finally Win getting the Juniors Cup for the whole state of Massachusetts."

"It seems to me things were quieter when I was young," said Walt.

"You're so old now," said Mrs. Hadley.

"I think that Tom's list of events isn't quite accurate," said Scoop.

"Why?" asked Tom.

"I think my scoop was the most important thing. It shows the superiority of mind over muscle."

"Ha," said Win, "if I remember correctly, it was your muscles that capsized that boat."

"Oh, that," said Scoop; "that just proves I can use my muscles with the rest of you gladiators if I have to."

"Good," said Matt, "we'll see you out for football practice Monday."

"Not this boy," said Scoop. "I'm going to write a novel instead. All about muscle-bound athletes who keep getting into trouble until somebody with brains comes along to save them."

"Seriously," said Ed Partridge, "if I live to be a hundred, which I plan to do, I don't think I'll ever see a more exciting bit of competition than that State Finals. I still can't get over it."

"It was something to see all right," said Tom Joyce. "I must say that Dan Slade put up quite a battle."

"I'll say so too," said Win. "I'm the one who can tell you that he did."

They were all sitting outdoors on the lawn behind the Hadley house. They had grilled their sizzling steaks, and now, with the meal over, they were resting and waiting to start a round robin on the croquet court.

"I hear that Dan came right up to you and said you were a better player," said Tom Joyce. "Is that true?"

"Yes," said Win.

"There's a lot of good stuff in that boy," said Tom; "I think he'll come around pretty well."

"Here we go," said Matt. "It's feel-sorry-for-Dan-Slade time again."

"I don't feel sorry for him," said Tom, "because I don't see any reason why I should. Why should anybody feel sorry for that boy? He has a lot to offer."

"I agree," said Mrs. Hadley. "If Owen Slade would just be a little easier on him it would be better."

"Does he play other sports as well as he does tennis?" asked Ed.

"He's one of my best athletes. Like Win and Matt, he's an all-around good one."

"Well," said Matt, "I finally got a compliment. It's about time someone recognized my sterling qualities."

"Your what?" asked Scoop.

"I won't answer that," said Matt, "because I know very well you have something nasty in mind."

"Not really," said Scoop and stood up. "If there's one sport I do like," he said, "it's croquet. It's a subtle game, tactics and headwork are very important. I challenge."

That started it and they chose up sides for a round robin tournament.

As they moved onto the side lawn, Dan Slade's big convertible slid to a halt in front of the house.

"Now what does he want?" asked Matt.

"I don't know," said Win.

"Well go see, Winfield Hadley," said his mother. "I don't care how you feel, remember your manners."

"I was going, Mom," said Win, and he walked out to the front gate. Dan was sitting in his car.

"Hi, Dan," said Win, "what's up?"

"I found my boat," said Dan. "I just thought I'd tell you."

"Great," said Win. "What shape was it in?"

"Not hurt too badly. I can fix it up all right."

"That's lucky," said Win. He didn't know what else to say, and then he noticed Dan watching the group on the lawn, a withdrawn look in his eyes.

"Dan, why don't you come in and have a game of croquet?"

Dan looked at him, startled, then looked away. "No," he said, "I'd better not."

"Why?"

"I don't know." He smiled a little. "I don't get along too well with Hughes and Slocum."

"You don't really know them. Come on."

"I'd better not."

"Well, okay if you want to be rude."

"What?"

"Well, Tom Joyce is here and my mother and Walt. You ought to say hello, at least, just to be polite." Win grinned.

"I guess I'd better at that," said Dan and slid out of the car.

They walked toward the group on the lawn.

"Dan came over for a game of croquet," said Win easily.

"Why now that's just fine," said Mrs. Hadley. "It's nice to have you, Dan. How's your mother?"

"She's fine, thank you, Mrs. Hadley."

"I haven't had a chance to tell you," said Ed Partridge. "That was some game of tennis you played in the finals."

"Thanks. I guess it wasn't good enough."

"It was darned good, Dan," said Tom. "How are you?"

"Fine, Coach."

"In shape for Monday's practice?"

"Yes."

The talk tapered off and for just a moment there was a small silence. Then Dan looked directly at Matt. "Hi, Hughes," he said, and added, "Hi, Scoop."

"Hi," said Matt shortly.

"Hi," said Scoop, just as tersely.

Tom Joyce stepped into the breach. "Okay," he said, "let's get on with it. We have to choose up sides again. Who's who?"

"You play this game, Slade?" asked Matt.

"A little," said Dan.

"You can guess who the champ is around here, can't you?"

"You?"

"That's right," said Matt, "so if you only play

a little you'd better be my partner. We'll clean up the whole group."

Dan blinked. "I'd like that," he said.

"Well, come on," said Win, looking fondly at Matt, "let's get going!"

The game started with a lot of noise and arguing and over it all Ed Partridge and Tom Joyce looked at each other and smiled.

It turned out to be a very pleasant evening.